"Have you worked in the desert before?"

Max Kramer's dark shrewd eyes rested penetratingly on Samantha. "Have you any idea what it's like out on those oil rigs? The heat? The primitive conditions? It's tough, Miss Whittaker. No place for a lady."

"Frightened of the competition?" she asked acidly.

The sharp planes of his face drew together, and the hot room vibrated with the strength of his anger and aggressiveness.

"I've no doubt you're fully qualified, on paper, at least—"

Samantha broke in, "You make it painfully clear you don't like working with the opposite sex, Mr. Kramer. Fortunately, I have no objection to working with men—*if* they know their jobs—and if they're intelligent enough to realize I know mine!"

Maelstrom

Ann Cooper

Harlequin Books

TORONTO • NEW YORK • LONDON
AMSTERDAM • PARIS • SYDNEY • HAMBURG
STOCKHOLM • ATHENS • TOKYO • MILAN

Original hardcover edition published in 1984
by Mills & Boon Limited

ISBN 0-373-02630-7

Harlequin Romance first edition July 1984

For
MEG AND CLIVE
and a thousand thanks to
BILL BARFIELD

Printed in U.S.A.

CHAPTER ONE

SAMANTHA saw the man striding towards her as she locked her car door. His was the only other vehicle in the hot, dusty car park. He was tall, aggressive-looking. Her skin prickled, sensing trouble.

'Do you work for Mepco?' he said, when he reached her. His voice was firm, his face and eyes hard; he was English.

Samantha stood her ground and stared up at him. 'And what if I do?' she demanded, hiding her surprise. Was the man clairvoyant? She was certain they had never met before. She would have remembered.

Shrewd, accusing brown eyes glanced from the top of her bouncing red curls down to her bare toes in thonged sandals. 'How long have you been out here?' he asked at last. 'I take it this is your first visit to the Middle East.' His eyes were crinkling against the early morning sun. Had he raced out of his car so quickly that he had forgotten his dark glasses?

'I've been in Dubai five days.' She took a deep breath. 'Now, if you wouldn't mind telling me who you are . . .'

'And in five days,' he interrupted, 'you haven't learned that women don't go round dressed like that.'

Samantha glanced down at her brief shorts and tee-shirt. Well, they weren't *that* brief. 'I'm perfectly respectable. It does get rather warm, you know, and I really don't see what it's got to do with you.'

He didn't enlighten her. 'But you're not in Dubai now. This is the desert.' He took a step nearer and she backed off. She couldn't stand him getting so close. '*You* may only be a visitor to the camel market,' he

7

continued harshly, 'but let me remind you that this is something that's been going on unchanged for thousands of years. These are men of the desert— proud, dignified, religious. To go into that market dressed like that, or practically undressed in their eyes—is nothing short of an insult.'

'How *dare* you!' But behind her anger she was appalled at her own stupid shortsightedness. He was right. Al Ain, and especially the camel market, wasn't cosmopolitan Dubai. She was a fool not to have realised it. But that didn't give him the right to march over and speak to her like this. 'And what do you expect me to do about it anyway?' she went on sharply. 'I've driven a long way, and I've no intention of going back home to get a long skirt.'

'Go and buy one,' he said, still with those hard brown eyes practically glued to her long legs and shapely curves; at twenty-five, Samantha Whittaker was no scrappy schoolgirl!

'Buy one? Oh!' For a moment she was silent. Why hadn't she thought of that? He went to turn away and she realised she still didn't know who he was or how he knew she worked for Mepco. But as he turned he suddenly seemed to notice the camera swinging beside her shoulder bag, and he turned back again—the lessons of the day were obviously not over.

'And don't go taking any photographs unless you're invited to do so,' he growled. '*You* might be a tourist, but these people aren't a tourist attraction. They're not some spectacle laid on for your benefit, they're . . .'

'I know,' Samantha interrupted, almost out of her mind now with rage. 'They're proud, dignified, *religious* men of the desert.'

'Right,' he snapped. 'Don't forget it!'

He stormed off, and Samantha fought her way back into the car, noticing with alarm that her hands were shaking as she tried to fit the key into the ignition.

And then she realised that behind her fury lay the beginning of the old fear; a tight, sick, icy horror. But she pushed it back, instead letting her anger take over, as she manipulated the unfamiliar automatic car into the drive position, and roared out of the car park.

The man was back at his own car now, and as Samantha shot past, hopefully covering him in dust, she noticed someone sitting in his passenger seat. It was a girl, a youngish teenager, with long dark, straight hair. It was a fleeting impression. His daughter, perhaps. Yet she wouldn't have considered him much over thirty-five. Obviously the wretched man had married young. For a second she pitied his wife.

As she swung sharply back on to the road, the air-conditioning began to work, and the icy blast made a welcome relief after the heat of argument and sun. But she forced herself to slow down, to forget about the brute, as she drove carefully past the thick throng of dark-skinned men and boys in dusty, flapping dishdashes. There were some goats being unloaded from a truck, skipping about friskily, a mingle-mangle of people, animals and parked vehicles spilling on to the road outside the entrance to the camel market. And then she was through them and heading back into Al Ain—now where on earth were the shops? Would anything be open at this time in the morning? And then she suddenly remembered it was Friday. *Friday!* Everything would be closed. And of course that great bully had known it was Friday—he hadn't cared if she bought a skirt or not, he had just wanted to get her out of the way!

But she didn't like being beaten, so she drove slowly through the almost deserted streets, peering down narrow alleys as she passed, but the only life in Al Ain this early on a Friday morning seemed to be the hub of activity back at the camel market.

And then she saw a funny little shop tucked between a shut up garage and a driving school. There was a bucket of plastic flip-flops outside, some washing up bowls—and what looked like a child's dress on a hanger. So she parked the car in a bit of shade and wandered over, and inside the tiny clutter of a shop there were two or three cheap kaftans, one of which was a respectable dark navy with a white snowflake motif around the bottom. Snowflakes! But Samantha bought it, without trying it on, and the Indian shopkeeper obviously thought she was mad. But it wasn't going to fit anyway, it looked at least five sizes too big—but now let that big brown-eyed devil accuse her of displaying even so much as an ankle. Funny, how come she remembered his eyes were brown?

As she walked back over to the car she saw the bright orange sticker at the bottom of her windscreen. Middle Eastern Petroleum Co. It was a distinctive sign, allowing her into the office underground car park. So that is how he had known who she worked for. Samantha felt relieved that there wasn't a more sinister explanation—yet it still didn't explain who he was. But Dubai was a relatively small place, and as she drove back to the museum car park, and struggled into the kaftan, she resolved that before very long she would find out all about him. Next time they bumped into each other—although heaven forbid it—she would be ready for him.

All the rumpus—and the dress-buying episode—had lost Samantha only half an hour, so it was still a little before eight o'clock when she finally strolled back down the road and into the camel market. She was here! This was the real Arabia! A satisfied, excited smile softened her mouth as she allowed herself to be enveloped in the dusty, swirling mass. But the wretched man with the brown eyes had made her selfconscious. She was practically the only woman in sight, certainly the only redheaded one—and she felt eyes on her; dark, mysterious, desert eyes. Were they curious—or contemptuous of her soft European ways? Thank heaven she hadn't come in here wearing those shorts!

And then Samantha lost herself as she squeezed her way around, her eyes everywhere, absorbing sights and sounds; small boys with mischievous flashing eyes, selling bundles of green fodder or helping with the goats, and proud, olive-skinned men bargaining for animals; exchanging wads of money or greeting friends with a dignified embrace, their sun-weathered faces portraying the harsh beauty of the desert that had bred them. And swinging from their belts were the curly, lethal khunjars; reminders of their ancient, timeless inheritance. It was all a swirl of heat, long dusty robes, colourful headdresses and brilliant smiles. Someone with goats in a pen let her take a photograph, and she smiled and thanked him, relieved that she hadn't upset anyone by taking a photo unasked.

She nearly tripped over the long kaftan once or twice, but the inconvenience was well worth while, in the circumstances. She had seen one or two women now, in black, all-concealing robes, with the distinctive leather beak covering nose and eyes. The thought of her tee-shirt and shorts beneath her kaftan made Samantha feel even more hot! And then at last she saw the camels loose in a large pen in the centre of the open-air market. She peered through the wire, fascinated, as men inside inspected the animals and marked the ones they had decided to buy with a brightly coloured aerosol spray. Now *that* hadn't been going on for thousands of years, she thought with relish.

And then she saw him, over the other side of the enclosure, staring past the camels and looking straight at her. It was the man from the car park—and the dark-haired girl. Was he surprised that Samantha was still here? Had he thought she wouldn't be able to track down a long dress? He was wearing his dark glasses now, but even from this distance Samantha knew he was watching her. She shivered and purposely turned away; if he disapproved of the market being used as a tourist attraction, then what was he doing here?

This time it wasn't so easy to forget him. As she wove her way back through the tightly packed throng, she kept getting a glimpse of a dark auburn bare head—perhaps with luck he would get sunstroke!

For another half an hour Samantha played an unofficial game of dodge, but she kept seeing him, once he was bending his head to catch something his daughter said, and another time, seeing a line of tiny children being led on a long piece of string, he actually laughed, and Samantha had almost collided with him head-on in the crush and the sound of his laughter had caused her heart to start banging. There had been another time, another place—and laughter . . .

It was after nine-thirty, she had been wandering round for ages now and it was getting hotter by the minute. And she had been up since five for the drive down from Dubai. Breakfast called—and the cool interior of a smart hotel. The men in the office had recommended the Hilton, so Samantha reluctantly left the market and plodded back to the car. If she didn't sit down soon she would fall down. Maybe after a couple of weeks she would begin to get used to the heat.

If she had not yet become acclimatised to the heat, five days had been plenty of time to discover that Arabia was a land of contrasts. After the heat, brilliance and chaos of the camel market, the hotel welcomed her with cool, tiled floors, lush green plants, tinted windows and the refreshing sound of cascading water. Breakfast was a lush buffet affair with unusual extras like yoghourt and dried apricots. It was all delicious, and Samantha tucked into it, only now realising how hungry she was, beginning to feel better by the minute.

She sat out of sight in a quiet corner, watching the Arab and European business men at the other tables intent in subdued conversations. In here the discreet headdresses and glowing dishdashes were a spotless white, contrasting with the dark business suits. Everything was touched by an underlying current of wealth which seemed to be a mixture of supreme confidence, slim gold watches peeping out of sleeves, and the display of expensive American cars outside.

Samantha sat back, cooling off nicely now, and sipped her orange juice. These past five days had taken a lot of coping with. A new job, new responsibilities, new people to meet. But wasn't that part of the challenge? The whole point in her getting a master's degree in petroleum engineering was so that she could come out to a place like this and use it. She could make good money working out here. Maybe save up and buy a little place of her own. Be independent. Never again would she rely on someone. She was finished with men.

Her glance rested on the profile of the handsome Arab at the next table, and there was something about him that suddenly reminded her of . . . She looked away quickly, swallowing as her heart started pounding in sudden panic. Stop it. All that's past. Heavens, was it really over a year ago . . . And then, over at the entrance, she saw someone else she wanted to forget: the man from the camel market. Did all the Europeans end up in the Hilton for breakfast? And he was alone; there was no sign of his daughter. And damn, the waiter was showing him over to a table right in her line of vision. If he sat down with his back to the window they would be staring at each other. And of course he did, but he hadn't seen her yet, the waiter was still in the way. Samantha sank into the corner of the high-backed bench, but there was no getting away, and as the waiter left him she found herself staring into the strong, sunbronzed face with the dark assessing eyes. He wasn't good-looking—or was he? His brows were dark and straight, drawn together now in a slight frown, his chin was tough, determined, his lips generous—but suggesting disapproval as he suddenly saw her sitting there. His hair was a dark, dark auburn, tumbled about. A visit to the hairdresser wouldn't have come amiss.

Somehow Samantha managed to drag her eyes away, but not before she had seen the disapproval leave his mouth and the corners of his lips begin to smile. Did he think she was interested? Huh! Little did he know. And then he was standing up, smiling properly, as the girl joined him again. Her dark hair hung long and straight to her waist. She looked interesting—Oriental. So she wasn't his daughter. Not because of her Oriental good looks, but because he had stood up when she had approached the table—and no father ever did that!

The waiter arrived to ask if she was ready for coffee, and as he cleared her table, the man and girl walked over to the help-yourself buffet table and somehow Samantha's eyes followed him round, tight white jeans and blue and white sports shirt doing incredible things for his shape. She could tell he was over six feet—well built without being overtly muscular; the shoulders and chest were broad, the stomach flat, hips narrow, thighs firm . . . Her stomach gave a strange twist and her fingers were shaking as she finished her orange juice. She had met his type before—and how! They thought they were God's gift to women. 'You can't go on like this, Samantha. Let me help you. It's for your own good. *Your own good* . . .' Even now the old voice could torment her. She had to get out of here—away from the man who had brought everything back.

'I've changed my mind—I don't want any coffee,' she told a surprised waiter. 'I'll just have the bill, please.' But to get out she had to pass the buffet table, and the wretched man was in the way. As Samantha approached he stretched for something in the centre of the table and his short shirt pulled out of the back of his jeans, displaying a tantalising strip of smooth, firm, suntanned back. Samantha felt her fingers tingle . . .

She was just edging past when he stood back, they collided and she would have tripped over the hem of the long kaftan if he hadn't quickly caught her with his free hand.

'Well, hello again,' he drawled, holding her against him for support several seconds longer than was necessary. She pulled away and glared at him, mad with herself for hardly being able to breathe. 'Saving your thanks for later?' he added, in a deceptively sleepy voice when she didn't speak. But there was a dangerous light in his eyes that spoke of more than anger.

'You want to look where you're going,' she snapped, still feeling the pressure of long fingers around her arm, feeling the same old panic . . . 'Let me go!' she hissed, the colour draining from her face, and for a moment he hesitated as those shrewd eyes seemed to swallow her up. Then he shrugged and released her—and, breathing a sigh of relief, she fled. Why, *why*, when she thought she was cured, did she have to go and meet such a brute?

She managed to pay her bill and get outside without falling over her kaftan again. As she pushed open the hotel's swing doors, the heavy heat hit her full in the face—and her sunglasses steamed up! She had to take them off for a moment. Boy, it was hot! But the car soon cooled down and the tinted windows were a relief, and soon she was heading back through the desert to Dubai, her breathing steadier now, the long empty road stretching soothingly between giant, twisted sand-dunes whose dainty, wind-rippled surface was now and then peppered with a line of camel's footprints. Or should that be hoofprints? She smiled, feeling better now, and stopped to take photographs.

It was after lunch by the time she reached Jumierah, Dubai's fashionable suburb, although she didn't live in the very best part of it. She shared a small bungalow with the other petroleum engineer on what Mepco called a twenty-eight-day back-to-back. While she was here in Dubai he was on leave in England, and after four weeks it would be turn and turn about. It had been strange to arrive last Sunday and take over a home that appeared to belong to someone else. There was food and bottles in the fridge, male paraphernalia in the bathroom. But at least the bungalow had two bedrooms, so that was one thing they didn't have to share!

On arriving back, the first thing she did was to shake herself out of the wretched kaftan, put the kettle on for a cup of tea, then pick up the phone. The telephonist at Mepco put her straight through to Frank.

'I'm back,' she said, stretching out on the sofa and crossing her fingers. 'Do you want me to come in?'

'So you didn't get bought by a white slave trader,' the American voice drawled.

'Couldn't persuade one to take me,' she said, trying to sound upset.

'Enjoy yourself?'

'It was great. Thanks for giving me the time off.'

'Make the most of it,' he said. 'I think we're on our way.'

'You mean the well?' Samantha sat up straight.

'Yeah. John's geology report came through this morning. He says we'll probably be ready for drill stem testing towards the end of next week.'

'Good.' Samantha was doing rapid calculations in her head. Ten days before the test to determine if this well was going to be financially viable, or not. And it would happen while she was the engineer on duty. 'I'll organise things right away,' she went on. 'Who's our service company? I'll contact them and get things set up—maybe tomorrow?' Drill stem testing was a specialist operation and wouldn't be done by any of the contract crews already on the drilling rig.

'It's been done, Sam,' said Frank. 'You see the guy tomorrow, if you want to. Nine-thirty. His name's Kramer.' Frank sounded tense, but maybe it was her imagination. 'Max Kramer.' He gave her the address and she scribbled it down. 'No need to come in now. Have you got everything you'll need for the morning?'

Samantha eyed the huge pile of paperwork she had brought home to study that represented all the work on this well, right from the very first geological survey. 'Everything,' she said, 'except John's latest report.'

'I'll get him to drop it in to you on his way home.' And then with a complete change of subject, he added, 'How was the car?'

Samantha laughed. 'I made it back here in one piece.'

'That bad?'

'It did sound rather strange once or twice.'

'Don't worry,' he said. 'The garage phoned—they're bringing yours back tomorrow.'

'Is it four-wheel-drive?' Although it was 'hers' she hadn't actually seen it yet; the other engineer had 'modified' it around a keep-right sign, and it had spent over a week in the body shop.

'Of course it's four-wheel-drive,' said Frank. 'You can't wait to get out there, can you? But make sure you can handle the thing before you drive in the desert,' he ended soberly, and Samantha didn't comment; sometimes she could hold her tongue for the sake of peace! And she wasn't quite sure how far Frank Douglas's humour stretched; his gruff cheerfulness would sometimes change into an almost surly introspection.

So, suddenly realising she had the rest of the day off, she showered and slipped into a green strappy sundress which was loose and cool and showed the beginnings of a suntan. She sat in front of the mirror piling on lashings of moisturiser, then rubbing plenty of conditioner into her damp hair. She would have a nice relaxed afternoon, going over the reports for tomorrow's meeting with this Max Kramer . . . She blobbed another spot of cream on the end of her nose that looked a bit red after this morning's walkabout . . . And she stared at her reflection, at the short, loose, wayward red curls, at her huge green eyes and neat little nose—her nose was all right. But her mouth was far too big for her small elfin features. A generous mouth, Bob had called it—but she didn't want to think about Bob . . .

John Trent, Mepco's geologist, turned up mid-afternoon with his latest report and they chatted about it for a while over an early gin and tonic that Samantha had pinched from her housemate. She must find out soon how one went about buying liquor—she knew it was legal, but complicated, and at this rate she would have quite a bit to replace!

Samantha liked John. He was tall and rather shy, not much older than herself, with a new wife, and they lived half a mile away in another Mepco rented bungalow, like hers, one of the small bungalows built at right angles to the sea. It was only the very up-market property that backed straight on to the beach, and Mepco didn't have that sort of money to throw away on its junior staff.

'We're having a bit of a party tomorrow night,' said John, refusing another drink and deciding he had better be getting along home. He wore steel-framed glasses and had smooth, short, dark brown hair. Somehow he always reminded Samantha of a serious badger. And he wasn't aggressive—that was what she liked most about him. 'Would you like to come?' he was saying now, probably wondering why she was smiling. 'Kate's dying to meet you—makes a change from the same old faces . . . No, I didn't mean . . .' he stumbled, suddenly realising what he'd said, but Sam just laughed, and knew it would do her good to get out—but there was no way she was going to get involved with anyone again.

She saw John out, then settled down on the settee with his report, but after a while she found her concentration wandering, instead seeing a time when she had been very much involved—when she had been engaged. How happy she had been then, how young and gullible. She hadn't even seen the other girl stealing her fiancé right from under her nose. She had been busy—newly qualified, working for an English petroleum company on the south coast. And this other girl didn't have a career, she had always been available, until Bob had begun to compare . . . and perhaps the idea of a working wife hadn't appealed to him—or maybe he just hadn't loved her enough. He had been sorry. Sorry! And her life had fallen to pieces. How long ago was that now? Two years! Good heavens. But Bob wasn't the problem, not any more. He wasn't the reason for those nightmares—that icy horror . . . Her hands started shaking and she cursed herself for remembering, for sitting here and consciously thinking about it. It was over. Nothing had happened . . .

The afternoon dragged on into evening and she was still edgy. She watched a film on television, then went to bed early. But she was still restless, frightened really of falling asleep—knowing what would happen when she did.

It began with the voice—it always was the voice. 'It's not natural, Samantha. Forget Bob. You *need* me,' over and over, 'you need me . . . you *need* . . ' And there was the dark and the hands on her clothes, on her legs . . . Pressing, insistent, and then the running, crying, lights flashing. Lost. Terrified.

Samantha woke up with a start, reaching blindly for the light, fighting with the bedcover. She sat up, breathing deeply, forcing it all away. It was the old nightmare. She hadn't had it for nearly six months. She had thought it was over. Damn. *Damn!* Now it would take her ages to get back to sleep, so she padded out to the kitchen and heated herself some milk. Her hands were still shaking, and she stood there, watching the milk—remembering.

'You need me—it's for your own good,' and she shuddered, remembering the man she had met at a party when she still hadn't really got over Bob, when she had been still emotionally involved. Her few dates with other men never came to anything, but she forced herself to go out, her flatmates had warned her not to mope about. So she had gone out with this fellow once or twice, and then he had taken her out to a country club for dinner, and then had driven home the long way, and had parked down a dark lane.

He had wanted to make love to her. Love! He didn't seem to know the meaning of the word. He had found out about Bob. 'It's for your own good,' he had kept saying, his mouth in her ear, his hands all over her,

her skirt sliding upwards, and she had pushed and fought and screamed, and in the end had struggled out of the car and had run along the dark, deserted lane ... And he had roared off in a rage, leaving her there, her bag still in his car—and she had been heaven knows where and it was past midnight ...

And that was when her real terror had begun. Five miles outside Southampton, in the middle of the black countryside, and at the end of the lane there had been just the dual carriageway, with lights flashing past her, shining on a solitary figure running down the grass verge. Never had she felt so *exposed*. Now, Samantha shivered at the memory, at the red, blinding panic as men stopped their cars and had offered her a lift. Had they thought she was crazy? And then another car had stopped and eventually she had realised it had a flashing light on the top ... The police had driven her home and had waited to make sure her flatmates were there to let her in. And that had been the end of it. They had changed the door lock. And as far as Samantha was concerned there would be no more men. She had started to look around for another job then. She had experience now. She was good at her job. Maybe she should have moved out of the area when she had broken up with Bob.

The job with Mepco had been a wonderful opportunity, working with them in America for a while—getting the reputation from the men in the office of being frigid. The ice maiden, they had called her, and the truth behind the silly joke hurt. Now that she had been sent out to the Middle East, she wondered how long it would be before the same rumour started spreading again.

The milk came to the boil and Samantha slowly poured it into the mug because her hands were still unsteady. Was that why she had applied for this job? Twenty-eight days here—twenty-eight days gone. She could always pretend there was someone special at home.

She pulled out a chair and sat down at the table, thoughtfully stirring sugar into her drink. No, that wasn't why she came out here. She wasn't running away. She was good at her job and she wanted to get better. She was happy, confident, with the work, even if a little on edge, because it still seemed a bit high-powered and strange out here. But that was no real reason to start having the nightmare again—she wasn't really under any particular pressure.

And then she remembered him again, the man at the camel market, the great brown-eyed brute . . . 'Will you stop remembering the colour of his eyes!' she told herself sharply. Then, cross, she took her drink back to bed, her hands steadying, and now she wasn't feeling quite so sick. It was nothing, a dream. So why did she still feel threatened? Why had the man at the camel market opened old wounds? Because he was big—aggressive? Because at breakfast at the Hilton there had been something in his eyes? . . .

She shivered, and felt something else twisting deep inside her. She had thought that Dubai was a small place—but it was filled with an awful lot of people, and she consoled herself with the fact that she was never really likely to bump into him again.

Max Kramer's office was in one of the tall blocks overlooking Dubai creek. Samantha drove in early, the bulky well file on the passenger seat, her mind already ticking over—wanting to impress. This was actually the first time she had arranged a drill stem testing on her own. Naturally it was quite straightforward, but . . .

So she had dressed with care. She could picture Max Kramer as tough, middle-aged, rather like Frank Douglas. Soaked in the oil industry—and a woman engineer might come as a bit of a shock. Although, naturally, Frank would have sorted that out when he had alerted the service company. But instead of shorts or a skimpy sundress, Samantha had chosen a thin cotton wrap-around skirt that swirled in creams and rusts halfway down her calf, and a matching, vee-necked tee-shirt in plain rust. Tall espadrilles made her long legs even longer, and as she parked near the Intercontinental and crossed the road, dodging back to front traffic, half a dozen heads swung her way.

The suite of offices was on the eighth floor and she was whisked upwards in a silent, carpeted, air-conditioned lift. When the doors opened there were acres of carpet and a reception desk, and an American girl with a surprised smile asked her to wait.

Samantha swallowed, feeling a bit nervous, as the girl went along a corridor and opened a door. 'The engineer from Mepco's here,' she said uncertainly, then came back and added, 'Mr Kramer will see you now.' He'd better, she thought, but just nodded a little smile and followed her in. 'He won't be a minute,' said the secretary, nodding towards another opened door, and Samantha realised Max Kramer was in there—she could hear the familiar tap-tapping of a teleprinter.

So she stayed where she was and stared around his office. It was enormous. Samantha took in cream leather settees, glass and chrome coffee tables, thick cream carpet, large overhanging pot plants. The whole of one wall was a huge tinted window overlooking the creek, and she strolled over to stare at dhows nosing side by side in the glistening heat. There was a desk in the office, of course, cluttered with papers. She wandered back from the window and stood in the middle of the room. How much longer was he going to be?

'Sit down—I won't keep you a moment,' said a

man's voice from the other room. Max Kramer? And then the machine stopped and she heard a strip of paper being ripped off. He was coming . . .

But she couldn't sit down, she couldn't even move, and she stayed in the middle of the room clutching her bulging file, her shoulder bag and sunglasses, her large green eyes rooted on the open doorway, waiting in agony for a glimpse of the man. Maybe her imagination was playing tricks . . . Remorselessly her heart began banging faster . . .

'Frank tells me this is your first trip in the U.A.E.' His voice was clearer, he was coming. But he was still reading his print-out—he still hadn't seen her.

Samantha gasped as he appeared in the doorway and he looked up at her quickly, the paper in his hand completely forgotten. Dark brown, unbelieving eyes stared at her—then his swift, penetrating glance swept round the office as if he expected someone else to be with her.

Samantha watched him in a tight agony of growing panic. It wasn't fair—it wasn't *fair*! She fought to control her breathing as his eyes snapped back to her again.

'You're *Sam* Whittaker?' he growled at last. Frank Douglas had a lot to answer for.

'Only to my friends,' she glared back. Why, oh, why did the great brown-eyed brute at the camel market have to turn out to be Max Kramer?

He looked appalled with the situation as well.

CHAPTER TWO

MAX KRAMER came into the room and closed the door quietly behind him; the secretary had vanished ages ago, sensible girl. His face was tight, hard, self-control measured every step. The white jeans and sports shirt had gone; today he was wearing pencil-slim dark brown trousers and a creamy silk shirt. It was smart, tailored, but casually opened at the neck. Yesterday's wayward red-brown hair had been combed into relative order, but it looked thick, inclined to curl, almost waiting for an excuse to go haywire. Samantha watched him with hostile eyes. He was a big man, tough, resourceful, ruthless; the kind of man who always got what he wanted. She felt a kick deep in her stomach.

'And *you're* Mepco's new engineer?' he said, and although he was struggling to keep calm, she could tell it was a big effort.

'That's right.' Green eyes flashed, warning him not to go further.

'You've a degree in chemical engineering?' And then suddenly remembering, he added with a wave of his hand, 'Please sit down.'

She sat! So did he, and they eyed each other across the giant desk. 'And a master's in petroleum engineering,' she said, because such a qualification was essential for her kind of job. He must know that, but for a moment she enjoyed rubbing it in.

He picked up a pencil and began banging the end down on his blotting pad. 'What experience have you had?' and because he was obviously a male chauvinist pig, his eyes veiled over for a moment, and he added, 'I mean in the oil industry.'

Samantha's lips thinned; she wouldn't be able to keep her temper much longer. Didn't he realise what an effort she was making as well? 'Enough experience to satisfy my employers,' she said through her teeth.

'Have you worked in the desert before?'

'No—and I don't see . . .'

'You don't *see*?' He threw down his pencil in disgust, scraped back his chair and strode over to the window. Samantha was instantly on her feet as well. 'Have you any idea what it's like working out on those rigs? The heat? The primitive conditions? It's tough out there, *Miss* Whittaker. No place for a lady!'

'Frightened of the competition?' This was crazy, she shouldn't be speaking to him like this. This was a fine way to start her career in the Middle East!

'Competition?' he repeated, as if he couldn't believe his ears.

Samantha took a deep breath. Okay, so it was a mistake to bring feminism into this. She was an engineer—doing her job. That was the only point of contact they had to have.

'Mr Kramer,' she began, trying to steady herself, thinking of Frank Douglas who had only made things worse by deliberately misleading Kramer into thinking she was a man.

'You were going to say something, Miss Whittaker?' Dark, shrewd eyes penetrated several layers of her skin. She took an involuntary step backwards, then hid the action by turning to pick up her file from the spare visitor's chair.

'Mr Kramer,' she began again, her face tight and her curls bouncing dangerously, 'you've made it perfectly clear that you dislike working with the opposite sex—but luckily I don't have a similar obsession.'

He raised both eyebrows.

'I don't dislike working with men,' she explained, '*if*

they know their job—and if they're intelligent enough to realise that I know mine.'

The strong planes of his face drew together and the room became alive with the vital rhythm of his sudden anger and aggression. 'I have no doubt that you are suitably proficient—on paper,' he said at last.

'On *paper*?' she repeated. Lord, the man had a nerve!

'But I thoroughly disapprove of women working in the field,' he went on, as if she hadn't interrupted. 'With the best will in the world you can only create trouble.'

'I resent that remark—most strongly,' Samantha broke in. 'Criticise my work by all means,' she added, her rage exploding near the surface, 'but only after you've seen it, and only *if* I do anything wrong.'

He stared at her, his brown eyes taking in her tall, slim figure, the tee-shirt accentuating feminine curves, the crop of blazing curls the colour of a desert sunset. A muscle in his cheek jerked, and she realised that same look had been in his eyes yesterday—at the Hilton.

'It is not my intention to be critical,' he said, taking a deep, steadying breath and coming back over to the desk. 'Perhaps I should see the well information.' He indicated that she should sit down again, and he did so himself, taking the heavy file that she slid across the desk.

'John Trent's latest geological report is on the top,' she said, in a sharp, snappy voice that didn't sound like herself. 'I'm sure you'll find everything all right with that!'

He looked across at her, then down at the report, obviously believing that such a stupid remark didn't deserve an answer.

Samantha's face tinged with red and she sat back in her chair and fumed in silent anger. Heavens, you read

about men like him, didn't you? But she hadn't really
believed that they were real. True, female petroleum
engineers were still a bit thin on the ground, but most
men liked the idea of a bit of feminine company out on
the rig—except that for a while they had to watch their
language. And after all, it wasn't as if she was expected
to stay out in the desert for long periods.

She watched as Max Kramer flicked back over
several pages, absorbed in the well file. His movements
were precise, controlled, his comprehension of the
situation instantaneous. As District Manager of a
specialist company like Gulf Services, he would be a
man to be reckoned with out here. He was in charge of
an operation that covered all the Arab states, she had
found that out from John yesterday. If there was
trouble on a rig Max Kramer's team were called in. He
had even been called in to help the experts put out a
well fire in South America. In this business Max
Kramer was important, and here she was arguing with
him on day one! The only consolation was that
when you were that big you didn't do the routine jobs
yourself. He would probably want to come out to the
rig and organise the drill stem testing, but it was
pretty certain he would assign the job to one of his
assistants—thank the Lord!

'Trent seems to think you'll be ready for testing in
ten to fourteen days,' he said, suddenly looking up at
her again, and somehow his penetrating eye-contact
was a shock.

'I'd say nearer seven to ten days,' she said. It was
just a feeling she had. The drilling had been going
well, there had been no snags—John was known to be
cautious.

Max Kramer nodded, then looked down again. No
questions? Was he going to take her word? Samantha
decided not to rely on it. But why all the hassle when
she had come in? Why had he been appalled at the

idea of her working for Mepco if he could accept her analysis of the situation as easily as that? And he was nodding now, flicking open his engagement diary . . .

'Today's Saturday,' he muttered. 'I'll come out with my assistant on . . . Wednesday?' He looked across for her consent, and she searched her own diary, fingers suddenly shaking, and said that Wednesday would be fine. 'Have you been out to the rig yet?' he asked, when he had scribbled the appointment in.

'I'm going tomorrow.' She was speaking more easily now, so was he.

'You're not driving yourself?' he said sharply. The slightly relaxed atmosphere hadn't lasted long.

'And what if I am?' Actually she was going out there with Frank and John, but she wasn't telling him that!

'Have you ever driven on sand—in the desert?' he responded.

'I told you,' she snatched her file back, 'I haven't been out here before. And at home they don't take kindly to your driving a car along a south coast beach.'

A little line around his lips turned white. He stood up as she did. 'How far is it? I mean—out to the rig.'

'It's thirty miles south of the Abu Dhabi road.' That much she already knew, or did he want her to give him a map reference? 'Not exactly the *middle* of the desert, is it?'

He came round the desk, tall and dark, etched against the huge tinted window. 'Miss Whittaker, do yourself a favour—go home.'

'What!'

'Thirty *yards* off the Abu Dhabi road can feel awfully lonely.' Strong fingers closed around her arm and she gasped before she could stop herself. He didn't seem to care.

'Are you saying I'll get lost—or are you hoping that I will?'

'It's a possibility.' And in case she should imagine

he was concerned for her safety, he added. 'Have you any idea what it's like organising a search party out here?'

'One thing I do know—*you* won't be heading the team,' she snapped, struggling out of his grasp at last and marching over to the door. 'I'll tell Frank Douglas he can expect you on Wednesday. Good day, Mr Kramer,' which, in the circumstances was being terribly polite, and she was halfway out of the room when he called her back.

'You forgot your bag,' he said slowly, dangling it from one finger, perching on the edge of his desk, looking dangerously pleased with himself.

Feeling a fool, she marched back to get it, aware of his appraisal with every step. 'Thank you,' she muttered, unable to meet his eyes, because somehow he was different now, taunting, predatory—very, very male.

'I suppose you're not going to take my advice,' he began, and his voice was husky as it ran along her nerve ends. Oh, he knew what it was doing to her all right. 'I suppose there's no chance of you going back to the U.K.?'

'None,' she retorted, taking the bag—but he kept hold of the strap; his eyes were suddenly little dancing devils.

'Then if I want you to stay out of trouble, maybe I'd better keep an eye on you myself,' he said, and she swallowed as panic began beating time with her pulse. His eyes had softened; they were deep, deep pools the colour of roasted chestnuts with long lashes curling thickly. 'I may object to you working in the desert, Miss Whittaker, but believe me,' he purred, 'I have absolutely no objection to your being here in Dubai. Come on,' he coaxed, 'don't look like that. I'm sure we could be friends if we—*really tried*—don't you?'

With luck the ceiling would fall down on top of him.

Samantha glanced upwards—but it didn't. 'I really
don't think that's very likely, Mr Kramer. Someone
who thinks me incapable of doing my job isn't the
kind of person I would wish to mix with socially.' It
was beginning, the dull, heavy pounding that spoke of
fear . . .

'A pity,' he said, looking not in the least put out.
'Perhaps I could persuade you to change your mind?'

Samantha took a long steadying breath. She had
dealt with this kind before; an employer or senior
colleague imagining they could get away with murder.

'Mr Kramer,' she began.

'Max.' His eyes flicked up and down, instinct telling
her that he liked what he saw.

'*Mr* Kramer,' she repeated, 'we don't like each
other. Fair enough—but let's leave it at that.' He had
released her by now, and she clutched everything in
front of her—it made a good barrier. 'Unfortunately
we shall have to meet from time to time,' she
continued loftily. 'You have a contract with my
company, which I'm sure neither of us would wish to
jeopardise. I shall only be in the Gulf on alternate
months, so a lot of the time you won't have to deal
with me at all. When we are compelled to work
together, *Mr* Kramer, I suggest we do so as calmly
and in as businesslike fashion as possible. Even then I
shall keep well out of your way—and I'm sure you
have every intention of keeping out of mine.' She
broke off for a moment, getting her breath back,
amazed that he hadn't interrupted—half expecting
him to do so now. But he simply leant back against his
desk, crossed his ankles, folded his arms, his face
impassive, his eyes enigmatic . . . But behind the cool
exterior she was aware of the rapid ticking over of his
computer-like brain. 'So shall we agree on that?'
Somehow she had lost the thread of her argument.
'Shall we agree to act like civilised people and keep

our distance?' She didn't go as far as holding out her hand to shake on it. Any overtone of friendship to this giant of a man would be a mistake.

'I'm sure we can agree on a lot of things, Miss Whittaker. Are you free for dinner tonight?' The mocking light in his eyes was reflected in the ironic twist of his lips.

'You haven't been listening to a word I've been saying, have you?' she retorted. Really, he was insane, flying in a rage with her one moment—propositioning her the next!

'Never mind what you've been *saying*—it was the delivery that interested me. Come on, how about it? Then perhaps a nightclub—a stroll along the beach . . .'

His words conjured up every romantic advertisement she had seen of a barefooted couple in evening clothes, strolling along the waterline at sunrise. 'And then back to your place?' she said, almost as cross with herself as she was with him.

'Definitely back to my place.' The smile was dangerously inviting.

'I know your type,' Samantha swallowed. 'You think everything can be resolved in bed.'

'Most things can,' he said calmly. 'And you're welcome—any time.' The firm lines of his face were etched with a subtle sensuality that she had never noticed before. Lord, he was lethally attractive, in a tough, earthy sort of way. How easily she picked up his electricity! Why was standing in the same room with him such a *physical* experience? She had the feeling that if she closed her eyes she would still be instantly aware of every silent move he made. It was as if they had been programmed to react to each other in this totally incomprehensible way. What, in heaven's name, was she doing even talking about bed to this perfect stranger? Hadn't she made up her mind never to trust a man again?

'I'm afraid you don't interest me in the slightest,' she managed to say, but she could feel her face flushing, could feel her control slipping away.

'And supposing I don't care if you're interested or not?' Max Kramer looked suddenly as angry as hell. 'Supposing we're not here in some nice cosy office with a secretary within shouting distance?' He caught her arm, strong fingers curling aggressively, while he wrenched her file and bag away with his other hand. 'Supposing we're stuck out in the desert—in a truck— alone? Cut off. And suppose I take advantage of our situation, what then—*Miss* Whittaker? How does your engineering degree get you out of that?'

'Do you think I need to go into the desert to discover how despicable men can be?' she said, although the words threatened to choke her. 'Is that what you're trying to do? Trying to scare me off? Imagining that I couldn't look after myself?' At the back of her mind was the crazy idea that he hadn't really been interested in taking her out to dinner—or taking her to bed. It was just a trap—but a trap that hadn't worked. Because she would always be able to look after herself. Always . . .

He kissed her, a long, hard, savage kiss that took her so completely by surprise that for several moments she couldn't even begin to struggle. She was crushed against the long length of his hard, unyielding body. One firm hand pressed into the small of her back, the other tangling into her curls, forcing her to return the kiss . . . The world started spinning; a dark world filled with the sound of breathing . . . and footsteps; it was her own breath and her own footsteps . . . She was running—and car lights were dazzling . . .

She was shouting something—thrashing out. The kiss was broken. Max Kramer was staring down at her with dark, disbelieving eyes. 'Let me go, you—you animal!' she sobbed, and she was wiping her mouth with the back of her hand, breathing heavily—beginning to shake now. For a dreadful moment she thought she was going to be sick.

'For God's sake, sit down.' He dragged up a chair and thrust her into it.

'I'm not staying—take your hands off . . .'

'What's the matter with you?' he interrupted. 'You're a dreadful colour.'

'It must be your fatal charm,' she snapped, but he didn't look convinced. In fact, he looked shocked—really shocked, and she could guess that the women in his life didn't react quite like that.

'Do you want a drink?' His voice was back to normal, controlled again. His breathing hadn't quickened at all. 'Water?' he suggested. 'A coffee?'

'I'm perfectly all right,' Samantha said, staggering to her feet.

'You ought to sit down for a while. Are you diabetic?'

'Of course not. I'm all right.' She collected her file and bag again. 'But obviously I shall feel a lot better when I'm away from here,' she added for good measure.

'Do you always? . . .' he swallowed. Was the Kramer ego actually dented? 'Shall I call you a cab?'

'I have my car.'

'Are you well enough to drive?' Brown eyes studied her face.

Samantha was feeling better by the second. 'I'll go along to the Intercontinental and have a coffee first.' He was obviously going to offer her one here again, but the look in her eyes warned him off. 'I'll tell Frank Douglas that you'll be coming out to the rig next Wednesday,' she said, loudly and crisply, as if they had just completed a successful business meeting. 'If there's anything more you need to know, please don't hesitate to contact my office.' She hoped he noticed that she didn't suggest he should contact her.

He nodded, still quiet with himself, as she turned and walked purposefully out of his office.

This time he didn't call her back.

'And don't sit there laughing and offering me coffee!' Samantha retorted, her green eyes flashing with a mixture of anger and amusement. Now recovered, she could even see the funny side of it. But she wasn't letting him get away with it. 'It's all your fault. Fancy telling him my name was *Sam*! You knew he detested women.' She took the coffee anyhow, and the corners of her mouth twisted wryly. 'You didn't have me bugged as well, did you? You wouldn't like a tape of the whole conversation?'

'Cross, was he?' Frank Douglas sat back in his chair, a huge, blazing smile on his face as bright as the sun outside.

'Cross! You could say that—if you were feeling charitable.' She flopped into the chair in front of Frank's desk. 'He wants to go out to the rig next Wednesday. Okay?' Frank nodded. 'You can do all the talking,' she continued after a moment's angry consideration. 'I think it would be better if I never speak to him again.'

'That bad?' Frank picked up his own mug of coffee. He was a big man, over fifty, she guessed. He was tough, weathered from thirty years in the oil business, but now his eyes and mouth showed the extra lines of tension. Frank was a man with problems; the office telegraph had told her that much—but Samantha didn't know any more.

'Have lunch with me,' he said suddenly, taking off his steel-rimmed glasses and tiredly rubbing the bridge of his nose. 'I could do with a few friendly smiles for a while.'

'Sorry,' she shrugged. 'I've booked some computer time—I'll have to work straight through.'

He looked philosophical about it, and for a moment she had the impression that he was a lonely man. 'Are you going to John and Kate's party tonight?' And when she nodded, he asked, 'Know where it is?'

'Vaguely.'

'Like me to pick you up?' Casually he opened a tall bottom drawer in his desk and brought out a bottle of whisky.

Samantha tried not to look shocked. Whisky at this time of day! 'Ah, yes, thanks—a lift would be great.'

He poured a generous splash of whisky into his coffee mug, then took a tentative sip. 'That's better,' he grinned, 'never did like my drinks neat.'

She tried to laugh, telling herself it would be a mistake to read too much into the little incident. The phone rang and she started to get up.

'Sit there and finish your coffee,' Frank insisted. 'After an hour of Kramer I'd need a darn sight more than that.' No, he didn't like Max Kramer; that was the second time she had got that impression. But now she knew why; how perfectly understandable.

The call was from downstairs, from the area accountant querying figures in a current contract. 'Okay,' Frank muttered, 'you'd better come on up— bring everything with you. Sorry, Sam,' he added, putting the phone down, but she was already on her feet. 'Money, money, money. In this chair you sure get sick of the sound of it!'

She could sympathise. Money was tight world-wide these days with the oil industry in the centre of the crisis. Never before had it been so necessary to keep exploration and production costs to a minimum. 'I'll go and play with the computer,' she smiled, but as she got to the door he called her back.

'Nearly forgot—car keys,' he said, jangling them at

arm's length. 'Registration number's on the tag. She's all spruced up and looking good. But you'd better get some practice driving on sand before you take it out to the desert.'

Samantha had every intention of doing just that; in fact, she had planned to find an empty beach on the way home.

'Kramer give you any other trouble?' queried Frank, when she had got as far as the door again.

Her first reaction was immediately to say 'no', but it sounded as if Max Kramer had that kind of reputation. 'Nothing I couldn't handle,' she said confidently, and Frank Douglas grinned.

'If you can handle Kramer, then I'd better watch my step!'

It was a joke with a serious edge to it. She laughed brightly and was relieved to be saved from further comment by the arrival of the accountant. She could tell he was the accountant by the permanent crease between his eyes!

As she wandered down the corridor to her own office, Frank's comment kept repeating itself in her mind. But *could* she handle Max Kramer? Was she tough enough?

It took four solid hours of finding her way around a new program before the disturbing question cleared from her mind.

Feeling calm for the first time that day, and also a little excited, Samantha left work at four o'clock and took possession of her own four-wheel-drive vehicle. It looked like a cross between a saloon car and a Range Rover. Very big—very impressive. It took a little while to sort out the lights and horn and the air-conditioning switch. Good, the radio worked . . . and eventually she edged her way out of the underground car park and headed for the Creek. Cars flashed past her, old taxis with the windows rolled down and the usual driver's arm sticking out; although whether to cool off or to make a hand signal, Samantha was never very sure.

Once over the bridge and past the docks, the road widened, traffic thinned, and soon she was approaching the wide intersection dominated by the new, magnificent mosque, all onions and lace, its intricate domes etched sharp and white against a vivid blue sky.

And then she was in upmarket Jumierah, where secret villas hid behind tall, obscuring walls; the wealth of their owners calculated by the number of security guards outside. On her right, between the low bungalows she caught glimpses of the bright blue Arabian Gulf, and snatches of a shining white beach . . . *Beach!*

Why not? Samantha did a speedy turn down the next right-hand opening between two opulent bungalows whose gardens backed on to the sand. She stopped at the end of the rough track and strolled on to the beach, the sand spilling into her sandals was red-hot.

There was no one about. No notices saying 'keep off'. After all, it wasn't a private beach, why shouldn't she practice her four-wheel-drive technique down here?

But she lingered a moment, screwing up her eyes against the glare, even though she was wearing sunglasses, and watched a large tanker slowly slide across the horizon. The sea was blue out there, a deep, solid, *rich* kind of blue, but nearer the beach it turned into an incredibly bright turquoise, before creaming milky white waves on to the pale sand. For a moment she forgot about the car and wished she had brought her bikini.

Reluctantly, at last, she headed back for the car, wiping her forehead with the back of her hand before climbing in. Switching on and easing the gear lever

into first, she slowly—slowly—edged on to the beach
... and very, very gracefully buried her wheels in the
sand!

'Oh no!' Samantha switched off and leapt out. And
she couldn't believe it. She was completely and utterly
stuck. The wretched thing had gone straight down—
and she hadn't done anything wrong—she *hadn't*. No
one could have been more gentle. Perhaps if she tried
carefully to reverse back out ...

But five minutes of the most delicate footwork, with
the perspiration pouring off her now, was only making
matters worse. She would have to phone a garage for a
tow. And she was cross now, really cross, as she
climbed down again and slammed shut the door.

And then she was aware of another car coming
down the side road. It turned into the garage
belonging to one of the bungalows. Perhaps she could
ask to use their phone.

She ran up to catch them before they went inside,
running fingers through her damp curls, aware there
were damp patches on her tee-shirt and that she
looked a bit of a mess.

'I'm dreadfully sorry to trouble you,' she said, as
the driver began opening the door. It was a man—he
was alone. The car had been driven in nose first, and
she was behind him ... 'I'm afraid I seem to be a bit
stuck,' she continued. 'Do you think I could use
your ...' Only she didn't finish the sentence, because
the man climbing out of the large black American car
was suddenly horribly familiar. Oh no! Not *him*! Why,
with the whole of Dubai to choose from, did Max
Kramer have to live here?

CHAPTER THREE

'You don't mean you just—just *drove* it straight on to the beach!' They were both staring at the marooned car now, and Max Kramer's voice was loaded.

'What was I supposed to do?' Samantha hissed. 'Pray to Allah first?'

'It couldn't have done any harm,' he responded.

'Oh—*funny*!'

'You are supposed to stop and *engage* four-wheel-drive,' he continued, wrenching open the door.

'What?'

'Didn't you wonder what that second gear stick was for? Didn't you read the instructions?'

'Who reads instructions?' Samantha grated. 'Nobody *said*.'

He passed a hand over his head. 'I suppose driving desert vehicles didn't come into your degree.'

She knew what he was getting at, all right. 'Look, it was a perfectly normal mistake. It could have happened to anyone.'

'But you're not anyone, are you? Tomorrow you could have been stuck miles off the road—risking your life.' Oh, he was enjoying this.

'Don't pretend you care!'

'Don't be childish,' he said, closing the door at last and striding back towards the bungalow.

Samantha ran after him. 'That's why I came here— to practise.' But he looked as if his opinion of her couldn't be improved, whatever she said, so she sighed impatiently, hating to ask him for any kind of a favour. 'If I could just use your phone,' and when he looked surprised, she added, 'to contact a garage.'

'There's no need. I'll tow you out.'

'No, I—I don't want to trouble you. Perhaps *you* would like to phone the garage.' Maybe it wouldn't be such a good idea to go into his house.

'You don't believe in doing things the easy way, do you?' Dark eyes licked over her. 'Want to come in for a drink while you wait?'

But Samantha wouldn't agree to that, saying she preferred to go for a paddle instead, and for a while she splashed up and down the quiet little strip of beach, trying not to notice her car at a funny angle, nor the heat, nor Max Kramer's garden on the other side of the low wall. She could see large sliding doors opening on to a shaded patio, then steps down to a pool and *emerald green grass*! There were flowering shrubs, all nameless to her as yet. She was surprised that things were still blooming in October; after a long stifling summer she would have expected everything to be shrivelled up. Unless Max Kramer could afford a full-time gardener to keep endlessly watering . . . She preferred not to think of all the little luxuries Max Kramer could afford.

At last she realised it was getting late, the sun was quite low, it must be getting on for five o'clock, and she was hot and tired and couldn't remember when she last ate.

Perhaps he hadn't phoned! Perhaps this was his way of getting his own back. Typical! She marched up and banged on the front door; when he opened it he calmly pointed out the bell.

'They haven't come,' she said, ignoring his gesture, and trying to ignore what the sight of him was doing to her senses. He had changed into his white jeans and a light, soft, honey-coloured sweat-shirt. His hair was damp, he must have just showered. She could smell a faint tang of some musky cologne. 'I—I suppose you did phone,' she stammered, swallowing with difficulty.

'Out here things happen—*insh'allah*,' he drawled.

'But I'm not prepared to wait *until God wills*,' she snapped, and he was surprised she had picked up that much Arabic already.

'Come and phone for yourself,' he said, standing back and holding open the door. Behind him the hall was wafting out its icy air—inviting . . . So she stepped past him, knowing it was the wrong thing to do, but somehow compelled.

'The phone's through here.' He led the way into a low, cool sitting-room, with the huge picture window she had seen from the beach. But the room bore no resemblance to the small, utilitarian bungalow that had been rented for herself. Here there was space and tasteful decorations, finished with discreet luxury that spoke of many years of travel in the Middle and Far East. There were exquisite Persian carpets on the floor in a rich mixture of subdued turquoise, blue and green. Samantha was immediately conscious of her sandy feet—but there was nothing she could do. The turquoise of the carpet had been picked out for the plain, full-length curtains and cushion covers. The settees were off-white, the same colour as the walls. There was an ivory chess set, with a game in progress, on a neat little marquetry table. And hanging on the wall was a gold-encrusted khunjar, an elaborate version of the type she had seen worn by the men at the camel market. As she slowly crossed the room her eyes took it all in. There were large green plants, table lamps on sculptured onyx stands, and a beautiful Arabian antique coffee pot, its distinctive shape reconigsable from her shopping expeditions around the souk. Not that she would have been able to afford something like that!

Everything spelt quiet sophistication, tinged with the Oriental—the unknown. And anything unknown was dangerous . . . fascinatingly dangerous . . .

Max Kramer picked up the phone and offered it to her. 'Or shall I?' he said casually, and when she indicated that he should do so, he put the phone back on a low table, and with his back to her, punched out half a dozen numbers. 'There's no reply,' he said, holding out the receiver so that she could hear the ringing. 'Sit down, have a drink. I'll try again in a few moments.'

It seemed a reasonable suggestion, and it was so lovely and cool in here... 'Thanks,' she muttered, and he went over to a trolley and poured her a large gin and tonic.

She perched on the edge of one of the enormous chairs and he sank down on the settee opposite, long legs casually apart, one hand holding the chunky crystal tumbler, the other slung out nonchalantly along the back of the settee. He looked very much at home, very relaxed—very self-confident. Samantha twiddled her glass in her hands, acutely aware of his speculative gaze.

'About this morning,' he began slowly, and she found herself looking up into his eyes. 'Did I really upset you that much? Or do you have...' he searched for the right word, 'a problem?' And when she didn't answer, he went on quietly, 'Has this kind of thing happened before?'

'No,' she answered truthfully. Because she hadn't allowed herself to get that close to a man since...

'I'm really not that much of an ogre.' The strong face changed into a dynamic, mind-shattering smile. 'And I still think it's true what I said—I still think we can agree on a lot of things. Why don't we give it a try?'

'I believe you suggested dinner,' Samantha began, in a disapproving little voice, 'and then back to your place...'

'Not if you don't want to.' He took another sip of

his drink. And she stared at him. Surely this wasn't the same Max Kramer who had fought with her in his office this morning—who had just been out on the beach implying that she was all kinds of a fool. 'We could have lunch somewhere—go for a sail . . .?'

'I—I don't think that would be a very good idea. I don't believe in mixing business with pleasure.'

His magnetic eyes trapped hers with a dangerous light. 'So you imagine it might be a pleasure,' he said, as if he couldn't help himself.

Samantha was totally and utterly confused. Yes, for an incredible moment she could conceive that it would be a terrific idea. For a moment she had wanted to say yes. Was she out of her mind? They both knew what would happen if he started getting close . . . And—she didn't *like* him, did she? But a quick glance under her lashes made her wonder if *liking* came into it. He was a lethally attractive man. Somehow he combined a wild, outdoor toughness with the intelligent sophistication of an educated, experienced mind. It was a dangerous mixture . . . She swallowed and took another sip of her drink.

'Perhaps you ought to phone again,' she muttered, really for something to say. So Max Kramer picked up the phone again and punched out the number. He didn't have to look it up—it was probably his own garage, he must know the number well.

'Still no reply,' he said, holding out the receiver again, and he kept it there for quite some time, so that she shouldn't think he was being too hasty. She even had the impression that he was being—nice. Actually wanting to put her at her ease. Really wanting to be friendly. 'Are you sure you wouldn't like to have lunch some time?' he asked again, finally putting the receiver back and picking up his drink again.

'I don't think I'm ready to start dating . . .' she

began, but then broke off at the sound of a door opening somewhere along the hall.

'Ready?' He caught her ambiguity, and although his voice was soothing, she caught his impatient little glance towards the door. Someone was coming and he was annoyed at the interruption.

Quiet footsteps padded nearer, and then in the doorway was a vision that made Samantha's eyes widen in surprise. It was the dark-haired girl, who she had decided wasn't his daughter. *Wasn't his daughter!* How naïve could she be? This time the dark hair was wrapped up in a towel, and the girl was wearing only a short silky wrap embroidered with exotic pink flowers. Her scanty wrap accentuated dusky tanned skin, slim bare legs and fragile arms, and the outline of a very young figure. She had huge brown almond eyes and the stunning beauty of an Oriental. She was exquisite, exactly fitting into the subtle Eastern flavour of the room. And no, she wasn't his daughter—no father was ever smiled at in that particular way. Which meant she was ... but she couldn't have been more than sixteen—if that. Max Kramer obviously liked his women young. But *that* young! Wasn't there a law against it? She put her glass down on the coffee table and was instantly on her feet.

So was Max. And he introduced the girl as Sue-Lee; there was nothing for the two of them to do except shake hands.

'You enjoyed the camel market?' Sue-Lee asked, with a shy little smile, and her voice was light and silvery, but with a husky little catch in it.

Samantha muttered something polite, knowing she just had to get out of here before she exploded. It was disgusting, obscene! Max Kramer was at least twenty years older than the girl!

'I'm in a rush,' she explained to them both. 'A

party. I'm being picked up at seven. So would you mind trying the garage again?'

'I can pull you out of there in five minutes,' he said, and his movements were suddenly quick, precise, adding something to Sue-Lee in her own language that made the young girl simply smile and drift away.

'There's no need,' Samantha insisted, following Max to the door. What had happened to the quiet few moments back there, when for a moment . . . ? 'If you'd just phone the garage.'

'Forget the garage—you're not in London now.' And he picked up his car keys and marched out into the hall. 'We can't have you late for your date. One that you are, perhaps, *ready* for?'

She resented his tone. 'My personal arrangements are no concern of yours,' she snapped.

'Whatever you say.' He opened the heavy front door for her; cloying, thick evening air wrapped a sticky hand around them. Samantha stepped outside, watching him warily. For a moment she had nothing else to say.

It took only five minutes for him to find his tow-rope and attach it to her car. Then slowly, ungraciously, he pulled it out backwards. Samantha sat up at the wheel, ineffectual, feeling a fool really . . . and then, thank heavens, she was back on the road. Max was climbing out of his car—walking back to her. It was almost dusk.

'What do you do—next time?' he asked, opening her door as she switched on the engine.

'I know—*engage* four-wheel-drive.'

'Let me see you do it.' Dark eyes were mobile, almost level with hers.

'Look, I'm not simple . . .' But he wouldn't move until she had done so, and it took a couple of goes to manipulate the little stubby gear stick.

He was finally satisfied. 'Goodnight,' he said, with

the old anger back in his voice. Obviously Max Kramer couldn't be nice for very long. 'Enjoy your date. Let me know when you're "ready" for me.' And he had slammed the door shut before she could think of a suitably cutting reply.

Cheek! He had a nerve! Wretch. Egotistical, chauvinistic *lecher*! Seducer of young girls . . . And even through her anger she was aware that that was what hurt most of all. As she bumped back on to the main road and headed for home, her mind was spinning with the arrogance of the man. Oh, why did there have to be a party tonight? She didn't feel in the least like going out. Now, where did she have to turn off? . . .

Somehow Samantha was ready when Frank Douglas arrived, although she was still screwing in her little earrings as she ran to the door.

His smile was tense as he greeted her, and his large, bulky presence seemed to fill the little sitting-room when she left him there to go and put a few bits and pieces in her little bag.

In her room, she gazed critically at her reflection. Not bad—considering the rush she had had to get ready. She was still fairly pale, ccompared to the others, because her fair colouring made it essential to take the tanning process very slowly. But the emerald green dress set off her eyes and blazing curls in a quite presentable manner. It was a loose, swirly dress with thin little shoulder straps—comfortable and cool in a crinkly cotton. She wasn't sure what everyone wore at parties out here, and she didn't want to appear overdressed.

Frank seemed to approve, anyway. Her tall spiky sandals brought her just on a level with his chin. 'I guess I'm taking the prettiest girl to the party.' And although she laughed, she knew he sensed her reserve, and confined himself to talking about the Trents during the short drive to their home.

The bungalow was very similar to her own; smallish, tonight bursting with people, but it had been furnished with love and enjoyment and felt far more of a home than her little bare box. For a moment she felt suddenly depressed.

She soon lost Frank, who positioned himself in the kitchen in charge of the bar. John Trent found her a drink and introduced half a dozen people, and she was surprised to find herself talking to a doctor, a radiologist and one of the Sisters from the local hospital. She had imagined everyone at the party would be employees of Mepco.

'I'm to blame for that,' said Kate, when their hostess finally had time to join them. She was smallish, very slim, with swinging dark hair and a full fringe. 'I'm not the lady of leisure that John would like to think. I run the body scanner at the hospital,' she explained. 'You should see my department!' Her impish eyes widened in delight. 'Money no object, all the latest equipment.' And as the others joined in, Samantha stood back and listened, and began to enjoy herself.

At about midnight, when some of the people were beginning to leave, John suggested going on to a night club.

Samantha wasn't particularly bothered, she had a heavy day tomorrow. But as Frank was giving her a lift home, and he seemed all in favour of the night club idea, there wasn't much she could do about it, anyway. A few people cried off, but in the end about ten of them piled into two cars. Frank was driving one of them, and Samantha began wondering just how much he had had to drink tonight.

But they drove into town without mishap. How warm it still was even at this time of night! How on earth could anyone manage without air-conditioning? What had seemed a luxury at home was definitely essential out here.

They discovered the place was rather crowded, when they had signed themselves into the night-club, and had all become instant members. The drink question had been one of the things Samantha had checked up on before she came, and apparently, although Muslims didn't drink, the ruling family had no wish to put similar restrictions on their visitors. Although it might have been a good idea if someone had put a restriction on Frank right now. He had grabbed one of the other girls and had fought his way on to the packed dance floor, gyrating and twisting with the best of them ... After a while their order came, lethal concoctions in fancy china pineapples, and Samantha sipped hers tentatively through a straw. Mm, not bad—in fact, rather nice. But she must make this her last.

Drawn like a magnet with the arrival of the drink, Frank came and sat down, retrieving his own drink from the selection on the table, and squeezing himself in beside Samantha and patting her hand.

'Enjoying yourself?' he muttered, pulling out a handkerchief and wiping his face. 'She sure is some little mover,' he added, eyeing up the girl he had been dancing with, and then catching a glimmer of disapproval on Samantha's face.

So he turned away from her and started talking to one of the men, and Kate Trent found a space the other side of Samantha, and seemed ready for a chat.

'He needs cheering up,' she explained, her words drowned in the heavy music. 'His wife wants him to go home—take a desk job. She flew back to Houston last month to try and persuade him to change his mind.'

'Oh,' said Samantha, feeling a bit ashamed of her

uncharitable notions. That was the problem with other people, they usually had as many problems as oneself—and were just as good at hiding them.

'He's missing her,' Kate went on. 'That's why we had this party today instead of the weekend. It's his birthday, but he doesn't want anyone to know.'

'That's sad,' said Samantha, and Kate laughed.

'Don't let him hear you say that!' And then she asked how Sam was enjoying her job so far, and before long the two girls were lost in fascinated explanations of their own careers.

John interrupted after a while, intending to ask Kate to dance, when suddenly he looked beyond their heads towards the entrance, where a couple of people were arriving.

'Say, there's Max,' he said. 'Let's invite them over.'

Samantha felt all the skin down her back prickle. 'Small place, isn't it—Dubai?' she said, with a tight little smile, but Kate didn't really know what she was getting at.

'Dance?' It was Frank this time, already tugging at her arm, and this time she was more than happy to join the heaving mass on the floor. The Filipino band were playing something slow, and Frank seemed glad to hang on to her; in the end she was more or less propping him up.

'Our friend seems to have survived his interview with you,' he mumbled into her shoulder.

'I didn't think the Company would like me to annihilate him on the spot,' she tried to joke. 'Not before the stem-testing, anyway.'

He chuckled and stumbled slightly, and Samantha automatically clutched him nearer. 'Guess we'd better sit this one out,' he said, and she laughed brightly, letting him lean against her, looking as if she was having the time of her life, as they swayed back to the table.

There had been a rearrangement. More chairs had been found, another round of drinks had appeared, and the space directly opposite her own was now filled by Max Kramer.

They eyed each other.

'Say, Max, this is——' John began.

'We've already met,' Samantha said hurriedly, forced to give Max some sort of social smile. The girl at his side frowned, until he offered the group an explanation. Then he introduced the gorgeous blonde. Her name was Jessica. Samantha wondered what had happened to little Sue-Lee.

Jessica smiled round at them all, but her eyes were cool when they reached Samantha. She was wearing a bright, razzamatazz dress in different shades of silk. Samantha was already learning that people dressed up for the evening, far more than back home.

Everyone began talking in little groups; John looked as if he enjoyed chatting up Jessica, Max seemed to know the doctor from the hospital where Kate worked, and Samantha chatted to a slightly glazed Frank. Lord, he was going to have some hangover in the morning!

'Would you give up your career for a husband?' he asked suddenly, and she was surprised that his speech wasn't even slurred.

'Would I do what?' she asked, trying to play for time, remembering what Kate had told her about his wife . . .

'Give up your career,' he repeated, 'if you got married.'

'No, of course not.' But she couldn't very well add that she had no intention of ever marrying. 'But I suppose if I *did*—marry, I mean,' she went on reluctantly, 'well, I'd have to take my husband's wishes into consideration.'

'So you would give up your career,' he said triumphantly.

'I *don't* mean that,' she said firmly. 'Considering isn't the same as totally giving way. I suppose I mean there has to be give and take.'

Frank laughed, and put a heavy hand around her shoulders, but she was aware of a line of bitterness around his mouth. 'When you've been married as long as I have you'll know that it's usually one person doing the giving—and the other one doing the taking.'

'I really couldn't say.' Samantha felt embarrassed that he should talk to her this way. After all, he hardly knew her. Or was that why? Was it easier to talk to a stranger? Or was it the half a bottle of whisky that he must have drunk by now?

But as her mind pondered on the problem, she glanced across at Max who was still deep in conversation, and she thought, no—he wouldn't know the meaning of give and take, either.

'Come on.' Frank seemed to have lost his melancholia. 'Let's have another dance.' And as they left the table it seemed to be a signal for the others to pair up too. Jessica began dancing with John, she noticed, and Max was leading Kate on to the floor. They danced well together. Kate flirted with him outrageously as they gyrated around each other. Max moved well, narrow hips rhythmically swaying in time to the beat. A relaxed, easy smile on his face as he chatted with Kate. He had arrived wearing slim dark trousers, white dinner jacket—the lot. They had obviously been somewhere quite smart. But now the jacket and bow tie had gone, the silk pleated shirt was open two or three buttons down his chest. All formal elegance abandoned for the music's sensual throb. Yet still he retained that indefinable something—that vital, sophisticated masculinity—that made him stand out among all these men.

Somehow Samantha forced herself to look away,

and she was just in time to catch Frank as he stumbled.

'Do you mind if we sit the rest of this one out?' he said after a few more moments, and when he had seen her back to their deserted table, she decided that it might be a good idea to disappear for a moment, herself.

'I keep meaning to say,' Kate began, as they met at the powder room mirror. 'I don't suppose you have access to a swimming pool.'

Samantha blotted her lips and started looking for her comb. 'Mepco doesn't run to those kind of fringe benefits.'

Kate grinned. 'So John moans.' She poked at her face and automatically screwed up her nose. 'But we've got a very good sports club at the hospital that's open to family and friends. You're welcome to come along—I'm there most afternoons, after one o'clock. Don't wait for an invitation. John will tell you how to get there.'

'I'd like that—thanks,' Samantha began with a smile. Then she winced as the comb tugged her unruly curls, and peering into the mirror more closely, she added, 'You know, I think my nose is beginning to peel.'

'Dreadful, isn't it?' Kate moaned. 'I get through enough body lotion and conditioner out here to lubricate a battleship!' And they were both still laughing as they went to join the others.

There had been another rearrangement of couples, two or three had left, Jessica was dancing with Frank now, and John was waiting for Kate. As soon as she reached the table, he immediately whisked her off. Which meant that for the moment Samantha was obliged to sit down, and the only other person at the table was Max. She chose a chair as far away from him as possible.

His eyes were dark and sultry—watching her, and

Samantha felt her breath quicken. She had seen that look before, on other men. But the Kramer version was even more threatening . . . It suddenly became difficult to sit still, so she picked up the nearest glass, hoping it was hers. Sickness began churning at her stomach. He was nothing but a great predatory cat . . .

'Don't worry if you really think you're not ready for me,' he began, and his voice was dangerously silky. 'I always make it a rule to leave with the lady I came in with.'

Samantha glared at him. Was her fear that obvious? Out of the corner of her eye she saw Jessica's blonde figure, very swish, very with-it, a glamorous lady of the glittering town. And then again she remembered little Sue-Lee.

'Get around, don't you?' she snapped.

He raised his eyebrows but refused to comment, which made it worse somehow. Probably the whole of Dubai knew just how much he did get around. Her skin began prickling under the steady gaze of those long-lashed, dark brown eyes. In a minute she would have to leave . . .

'Like to dance?' he asked eventually, putting down his drink, as if she was bound to accept.

'No, thanks.'

He looked surprised—cross. Then his glance travelled beyond her to the crowd of gyrating couples. 'You only like older—*married*—men, do you?' he said nastily, his eyes fixed firmly on Frank.

That was just too much! How dared he? 'Look,' she began, leaning forward across the table and glaring at him with her big green eyes, 'I don't happen to think much of men—any man. Old, young, married—or single. I'm not interested, Mr Kramer.'

She scraped back her chair to leave, but he stretched out and caught her wrist. 'There's no need to leave. We don't have to dance. We can talk . . .'

'You may have noticed that when we talk, we argue.' She hated people grabbing her wrist, it made her go cold inside. 'Now, let me *go*——' and something of her rising panic seemed to get through to him. 'Tell the others I had to go—I've an early start tomorrow—today . . .' And for a moment she lost herself in the swirling crowd of dark couples spasmodically illuminated by spiralling coloured lights.

This was stupid—stupid. She was a fool to leave. But she had to get away. Away from Max Kramer. Away from those dangerous eyes . . . And at last she reached the door—and was free. But where now? The night-club was situated on one of the upper floors of a new, smart shopping centre. They had come up in a lift, around a corner somewhere. Samantha began hurrying along, aware that someone might be following . . . As she rounded a corner she heard footsteps behind . . . The place was deserted, all the shops closed . . . a strange, echoing isolation with window displays of Oriental antique furniture and Persian carpets. She dashed round another corner— she must have missed the lift, so where were the stairs?

'Sam! Samantha!' It was Max Kramer's voice.

Oh no! She ran on, her heels making a dreadful noise on the tiled floor. Around another corner, only some of these shops hadn't been fitted out yet, their fronts were still boarded up with the interior decorators' trade plaque nailed on to it.

It was a dead end. Trapped. Panic fought with iron self-control. She mustn't get hysterical. She wasn't miles out in the country this time. People were close . . . in the night-club. Only she didn't know where that was any more. She backed into a darkened doorway. Maybe he hadn't heard her come down here. Her heart was banging high up in her throat, surely he would hear.

'Samantha!' He tried again, and she heard him pause, as if turning this way and that. 'Don't be a fool—it's late. You can't go home alone . . .'

She pressed into the doorway, holding her breath, willing him to go away. But he started coming down the walkway. And suddenly she could see his reflection in the window opposite . . . Why couldn't that have been boarded up too?

And then he saw her, reflected in the same window, and now there was nowhere else she could go, and she clenched her fists as he came running up to her hiding place.

'And what was all that about?' he began, standing in the doorway, blocking her escape, and he was so tall and powerful—so damned aggressive.

'Get out of my way—go back to the others!' Frantic now, Samantha flew at him, trying to get past.

He caught her shoulders. 'What's with you?' For a moment he looked genuinely puzzled.

She hit him, her sense overwhelmed by the dynamic masculine aura that seemed to throb from the wretched man. She could smell that musky, virile freshness of an athletically fit body. Heavens, why was she even *thinking* like this?

'Let me go,' she tried again. 'The others will be wondering where you are.' Why wasn't there anyone else about? Why didn't someone try to stop him? For all they knew he could be attacking her. This was just as bad as being five miles out in the country on a dark night . . .

'I said, what's with you?' He shook her. 'Are you crazy, or something? Do you think this is the kind of town where a girl ought to be on her own at this time in the morning?'

'I can look after myself.' Everything started spinning.

'Don't start that again.' His voice seemed to be

coming from a long way off. She couldn't see him any more, yet he was all around her—overpowering her.

'Just get out of my sight!' she practically screamed, opening her eyes at last, while giving him an almighty shove. And when he obviously had no intention of doing so, she added almost hysterically, 'Can't you see I'm going to be sick!'

CHAPTER FOUR

'WHAT happened to you two? Samantha, you look dreadful!' Kate's provocative enquiry suddenly changed to concern.

'I'm all right now,' she said, aware that it must be pretty obvious what had happened.

'Never mind, you're allowed to go mad on your first night out in Dubai,' said John, patting her arm and explaining that he was driving Frank's car and Kate was following in their own. Max had been taking her back to the night-club so that she could sit down for a moment, but they had met the crowd already on their way out.

'I don't think I want to get into a car just yet,' Samantha admitted, so they stood her in the blast of the air-conditioning and she took welcome gulps.

Max was watching her carefully, her dark eyes enigmatic. He was keeping his distance. Since it had happened he hadn't touched her. And it wasn't because he was squeamish. He knew ...

'Next time I should take more water with it,' said Jessica, who had looked furious when she had first seen Samantha, but who was now laughing and slipping her arm through Max's. 'Come on, darling,' she said seductively. 'I've got to be up early in the morning ...'

'Was it the wine?' Kate broke in quickly, 'or have you eaten something? Maybe it's Rashid's Revenge.'

Samantha managed a weak grin as Max began backing away. But his eyes were still on her, and she looked at him unwaveringly and said, 'I'll be all right now.' Then someone brought out a chair from the night-club, and someone else was handing her a glass of water. 'It's the heat,' someone else was saying kindly. But Samantha knew it was none of those things. And Max Kramer knew it too. But as he disappeared with Jessica, Samantha started feeling sick again.

Luckily it didn't come to anything, and soon she was being driven home by John, with a jolly Frank in the back, calling, 'Make sure you're in the office by seven. You haven't forgotten we're going out to the rig?'

Samantha groaned. Two o'clock in the morning didn't seem an ideal time to contemplate the prospect. She guessed Frank wouldn't be sounding quite so bright then, either.

But she was wrong. Frank wasn't the Company's man for nothing. Thirty years in the field had given him a tough constitution.

Samantha was washed out, not hungover, as they joked, on a few glasses of wine. But her humiliating encounter with Max Kramer the night before had troubled her restless few hours of sleep. Perhaps if one of the men drove out to the rig, she would be able to have a little snooze in the back of the car.

But no such luck. Frank suggested that she drive, which was sensible really, to get her first experience of desert driving while not alone. Well, maybe not *quite* her first experience—but she didn't want to remember Max Kramer on Jumierah beach. In fact, she didn't want to think about Max Kramer at all . . .

It took a long time. They left Mepco's office by seven-thirty, and the Abu Dhabi road out of town was pretty clear, but once they turned off the highway and headed south into the desert, Samantha found the rough yet firm track needed all her concentration. The gully and dunes on either side looked like treacherously soft sand. But at least this time she had remembered to stop and engage four-wheel-drive!

It was nine-thirty when they reached the rig; she

hadn't realized it would take her two hours to do thirty miles. The two men piled out of the car, and Samantha waited a moment, taking off her sunglasses and slowly rubbing the back of her neck. What she needed was a large mug of coffee.

She had parked beside one of the Portakabins that Frank said was his office. It was covered with dust, the car was covered with dust, *everything* was covered with dust. It was all harsh, bright and real; a cluster of shabby Portakabins, trucks, chain, winding drums—the sound of men laughing, the continual grinding of heavy machinery. And the skeleton of the rig, towering over them like some prehistoric bird, the drilling platform quite high up—and over everything was the roar of diesel engines—a roar that never ceased.

Samantha put her sunglasses back on, grabbed her folder from the back seat and climbed out. God, it was hot! The sun beat back all around from the dry, parched ground as well as from the sky above. Was there such a thing as quadraphonic heat? She was still chuckling to herself as she went to join the others.

'So you want to pull a wet string after the drill stem test?' she said, looking Frank straight in the eye. After two coffees and a whirlwind tour of the camp, they were now around Frank's desk discussing the forthcoming stem-testing that would be undertaken by Max Kramer's specialist team.

'Have you any objections?' he asked, taking off his glasses and polishing them with a Kleenex.

Samantha rocked back in her chair, playing for time, not sure whether this was a normal procedure for Frank, or if he was testing her. 'String' was the jargon name for the drill pipe. Pulling strings was what would happen when Max's drill stem-testing equipment, attached to the end of the pipe, was eventually withdrawn. But to pull a *wet* string meant that the equipment would be coming up without the protection—inside the string—of the usual solution called mud. Mud served two purposes; its circulation brought to the surface all the samples for the geologists' analyses while absorbing any dangerous gases, and the hydrostatic pressure of the circulating mud, really a complicated mixture of special clays and chemicals, would keep the oil from gushing up if anything went wrong—and *if* there happened to be a fault in the blow-out preventers.

'You want to save time?' she asked at last.

Frank nodded as the softness of his cheeks seemed to tense. 'We can save a lot of rig time—and rig time means money.'

She looked across at John. 'And you want the reservoir sample uncontaminated, I suppose.'

'You've been making the reports,' he said. 'You told me this well looks borderline. There's going to be an awful lot of wasted money if it's decided it isn't going to be financially viable.' John's eyes were serious. 'And if that decision is made on the strength of my analysis—and on the strength of the sample Kramer can bring up—then yeah,' he nodded, 'I'd prefer not to have any mud down there.'

Samantha sighed. It was the old conflict. Mud, possible contamination or loss of the sample, slowness, *safety*—versus—a wet string, speed, clean samples—and danger.

'How important is the time factor?' she asked, looking at Frank again.

He grimaced. 'Vital.'

'Silly question really.' As she spoke, she flicked through her papers. 'There's nothing to suggest any unusual problem. With careful handling the risks should be minimal. Kramer's company is . . .?'

'The best,' Frank finished for her, although he sounded reluctant to admit it.

Samantha's mind was racing ahead, calculating risk against expediency. 'There's a hell of a lot of difference between running a rig on paper and actually operating in the field,' she had been told, while still at university. And this was perhaps the most controversial decision she had had to make. But she wouldn't be steamrollered into making the wrong choice just because she was a woman. She wouldn't be blackmailed into taking a tough line just to win their respect.

They were waiting for her; Frank tense, drumming a Biro up and down between his fingers; John professionally interested, and the big American tool pusher in charge of the drilling floor, who had seen all this before, but was enjoying the novelty of seeing a woman in the hot seat. Samantha was wearing a buttercup yellow, short-sleeved zip-up jump suit in cool cotton. It would have brightened the dullest London day, so out here it was positively sensational.

'Okay,' she said at last, looking up from her reports. 'It's a calculated risk, but no more than that. I see no other reason to advise against pulling a wet string.'

'Right.' Frank nodded, pleased with her decision, but perfectly aware that he could have overruled her on any account. As Company man, his word was law. Yet it would go on record that she had sanctioned it as well.

Everyone began scraping back their chairs, Frank suggested they all go up and have a look, and heads turned, and conversation stopped, as someone lent her a hard hat and gloves, and she began climbing the metal ladder up to the drill floor. Here everything was noise and movement; powerful machinery, powerful men, danger, excitement, the manifestation in stark actuality of all her analyses and graphs on paper.

She was introduced to the driller and his crew who could only nod hastily in acknowledgment, and she gazed upwards through the superstructure as another thirty-foot section of pipe was swung into place.

'How's it going?' Frank asked the tool pusher, who had come up to join them.

His experienced eyes were everywhere, watching the men wrenching on the giant tongs . . . 'Looking good,' he shouted back. 'Come down and look at the drilling reports.' But Samantha hung about until last, knowing she was only in the way—but might not be able to find the excuse to come up again for quite a while. As she scrambled down the ladder again, she tried not to think about the interested stares of the men staring up. They would soon get used to seeing her around . . . She jumped back down on the sand and pulling her hat off, wiped her forehead with the back of a grubby hand, and directed a long, cooling breath up her face. Boy, it was lethal up there! How could they stand working in that continual heat? Thank heaven, even out here the Portakabins were air-conditioned.

She was relieved when Frank took her over to her little office, which would double as a bedroom during the twenty-four hour-a-day stints she would sometimes have to make out here.

It was a small, *cool*, utilitarian room, with a desk, bunk bed, washbasin and cupboard which she opened and found a giant rubberised suit hanging up.

'These slickers might be all right for my opposite number,' she laughed, pulling them out and holding them against herself, 'but I think I'll have to find the smallest set they make,' and Frank laughed too, as the long legs folded down on the floor. Then she tried on the hard hat, and that came down over her ears . . . Job sharing with another engineer was the only way to survive in these conditions, but they both agreed that there were some things that couldn't be shared.

It had been a good day. Exciting, satisfying; a

challenge to see the rig and know that her recommendation would be a major factor in the decision
whether it would go into production or not. What a
responsibility! She hadn't actually made such a
recommendation alone yet. But that was her job. She
had been trained for it. At least this part of her life she
could approach with confidence.

John drove back, much faster than she had driven
out, and it was only a little after two when they
reached Dubai. Frank and John stayed on at the office,
but Samantha had done enough for one day, so she left
them and drove out to her end of Jumierah. Although
the air-conditioning had been left on and the
bungalow was comfortably cool, she didn't feel like
taking a shower and hanging around indoors, she felt
like going for a swim. Then suddenly she remembered
Kate's invitation.

There was no reply from her at home. Good, that
probably meant she was over at the pool. But the last
thing Samantha wanted was to do battle with the traffic
trying to find the hospital sports club, when she didn't
even know where the hospital was. So she grabbed her
bikini and towel and a few bits and pieces and strolled
back to the main road, which would be alive with taxis.

The journey was short, but Samantha was glad she
hadn't missed it. The old, dusty car was a vision of
ornate, plush decoration inside, and the handsome
young Arab driver, more than willing to have a
chat, seemed genuinely appalled that at her age she
didn't have a husband and half a dozen children.

Kate's name gained Samantha entrance to the sports
centre, and she was shown up to the open-air
swimming pool, surrounded by a high, concealing
wall. Sun loungers and umbrellaed tables fought for
the sparse shade, and waiters in smart black and
órange uniforms carried drinks and snacks to the few
people using the pool that afternoon.

For a moment Samantha didn't recognise anyone, until suddenly a girl was waving from the middle of the pool, then swimming across to the steps. Kate climbed out, the sun instantly ready to dry her skin, her dark hair coiled up in a topknot. She looked stunning, her superb tan accentuated by a brilliant turquoise bikini.

'I hope you don't mind me just dropping in,' said Samantha, when Kate had ordered them both a large orange drink and had pulled over another sun-lounger.

'Lord, no—delighted! I *said* just come.'

So Samantha changed into her own black bikini and had a quick shower in the changing room, catching sight of her reflection and wishing she had a good tan herself. Perhaps this new bikini was a mistake. It was only held together by thin little ties; a sudden move in the wrong direction could be disastrous!

'John said you were going out to the rig this morning,' said Kate, when they had had a short swim and their orange drinks had arrived. Now, with a towel protecting her toes, and the rest of her stretched out in a thin strip of shade, Samantha felt her late night and heavy day begin to catch up with her. 'Did it work out?' Kate added, stirring her rapidly melting iced drink with a straw.

'Mm.' Samantha rolled over and reached for her own glass. Normally she would have liked to discuss her work with a friend, but Kate might tell John and she didn't want anyone to pick up the impression that she was still a bit worried about this stem-testing. Although perhaps *worried* was rather strong. 'How about you?' she asked instead. 'Had many bodies to scan?' and Kate laughed and said things were pretty quiet at the moment, which probably meant that a crisis was just on its way.

They swam again and drank more orange juice, and Samantha chanced sunbathing for fifteen minutes, before fitting herself into the thin patch of shade again.

A few more people had arrived now, and Samantha creamed herself and watched the colourful, cosmopolitan group, waving to the handsome Persian doctor whom she had met last night at Kate's party—but who, fortunately, hadn't come on to the nightclub. He was here with his wife and two small children, his dark, powerful body slicing the cool water as he dived and fooled around in the pool. For a moment Samantha thought of Max Kramer; Max going off with Jessica last night. No, she couldn't imagine him as part of such a happy family group.

'Gorgeous children,' said Kate, sitting up and reaching for her suntan cream.

'Feeling broody?' Samantha laughed.

'We're supposed to be out here to save enough money to buy our own house. Children come later.' Her long dark hair had fallen loose, and as she twirled it back up on top, she glanced sideways at Samantha. 'Have you ever been married?'

'Do I look that harassed?' she asked, trying to make a joke out of it, yet feeling rather strange. Why had she suddenly gone tight inside?

Kate grinned. 'People usually come out here for a reason, that's all. Broken marriage—or love affair. The need to start a new life.' She laughed again. 'Or the need to earn some decent money.'

'I didn't exactly *come* out here,' said Samantha, for some reason immediately on the defensive. 'I was sent here—it's my job. Next year it might be America—England—or the Far East.'

'Sounds very glamorous,' said Kate, beginning to cream her legs. 'But I think you're brave. John's told me what it's like on those rigs,' and then she broke off, waving to someone. It was a tall, good-looking girl, whose dusky skin colour suggested she could come from somewhere interesting. 'It's Farida,' said Kate, 'our neuro-surgeon,' and seeing Samantha's surprise, she added, 'I know, looks too young, doesn't she? But she's thirty-two. Syrian—and brilliant. The hospital's lucky to have her.'

Farida came over. At close range her striking good looks were quite beautiful. She was tallish, and very slim, with dark hair scraped back in a severe style that somehow complemented her fine bone structure and delicate features. Her accent was gravelly and her smile almost shy as she was introduced. Samantha decided she liked her. Imagine being a brilliant neuro-surgeon at her age! Samantha mused on this as Farida dumped her bag beside an adjacent lounger and went inside to change.

'That looks like trouble,' said Kate, pointing to a helicopter slicing its way through the sky.

'You mean an accident?' asked Samantha.

Kate nodded. 'Off one of the rigs, probably. Maybe offshore,' She settled down again and reached for her book. 'No sense in worrying, we'll know soon enough if they want me.' And Samantha was just about to settle down as well when an ice-cold, wet rubber ring landed right in the middle of her stomach.

With a shriek, she jumped up, and the children were apologising in their attractive English, and laughing at the same time, and the Persian doctor with the beautiful eyes was climbing out of the pool to retrieve the ring.

'Maybe I don't want to give it back,' she said, for some ridiculous reason, and she held it behind her back while the children screamed at their father to go and get it. Her eyes flashed a wicked challenge and his dark eyes responded with a taunting light that was all their own. His experienced glance flicked up and down the tall, shapely length of her, and Samantha knew he liked what he saw.

She backed away, dangling the ring out of reach, and he was coming towards her, getting closer and closer, those mysterious eyes ready to eat her up ... And suddenly he grabbed her and they both struggled for the ring, and although the situation was spiced with a taunting sexuality, it was all innocent and perfectly safe because the children were there, and his wife—and she was laughing, and shouting encouragement, and Samantha wasn't really surprised to find herself being tossed into the water. She shrieked as she surfaced, swimming for safety, climbing out and running long fingers through her red curls. How good the sun felt, hot and drying on her cool, damp skin. She shook the last of the water out of her eyes and went to join the others ... But there was a man standing next to Kate now, and there was dark disapproval etched along the strong, familiar lines of his face. Samantha's stomach gave a kick. Wasn't it enough for him to haunt her dreams? Did Max Kramer have to haunt her days as well?

'What's he doing here?' she asked, as Max strode off to the changing room, and Samantha was stretching out on her lounger again. 'I thought this club was only for hospital staff.'

'And their friends,' Kate reminded her. 'He's Farida's man of the moment. Well, something like that. They've been friends for ages now.'

Samantha pulled a face. 'Likes variety, doesn't he?'

'You mean Jessica, last night?'

'I wasn't only thinking of her,' said Samantha, watching the dark-eyed children and suddenly re-membering Sue-Lee. 'There's that girl who lives with him.'

'So you've heard of her,' said Kate, never for a moment thinking that Samantha had actually been inside Max Kramer's luxurious bungalow. 'He says she's his ward.' Her paperback slid to the floor and she left it there.

'Ward?' repeated Samantha in surprise.

Kate grinned. 'He *says* he's her guardian.' She glanced towards the changing room as Farida appeared, but she went straight into the water, so they were safe for a while. 'But there are opposing schools of thought as to exactly what that might mean.'

Samantha remained silent, but her eyes coaxed Kate to go on.

'Some say she isn't his ward but his daughter. In which case, where is the mother? She must be very special if Max is taking care of Lee.'

'Is he married?' Samantha asked, feeling suddenly breathless.

'Not as far as anyone knows.' Kate fiddled with a strand of her hair as it began escaping again. 'And the other school of thought is that she isn't daughter or ward, but——'

'Mistress?' Samantha offered, and the other girl nodded. 'But how old is she?'

'Over the age of consent,' Kate said briskly, 'you can be sure of that. Max Kramer's no fool . . .'

Oh no, no fool. Just a despicable, womanising, chauvinistic lecher . . . Samantha fumed in silence until Max appeared out of the changing room and dived straight into the pool with Farida. She had had enough, and slipping on a light towelling wrap, she announced she would go back down and order them both a pot of tea.

But that strategy didn't work, because when she came back, Farida and Max were sitting with Kate, and Samantha couldn't join them, she just *couldn't*— so she slipped into the pool and began playing with the children, who seemed delighted with her company now that their mother had gone to sit under one of the coloured umbrellas, and seemed to be having an afternoon doze. For ten minutes Samantha acted like a child herself, aware, yet not caring, that Max Kramer was watching her. The little black bikini was a bit troublesome, as she had prophesied, and she had to keep stopping and hitching it together.

After a while she saw the waiter arrive, but he didn't have their tea. He seemed to be giving a message to Farida, and the two women were gathering their things together, looking as if they were about to go and get changed.

'Emergency,' Kate explained, when Samantha swam over to the side. 'Came in on the helicoper—head injuries. They want Farida—and she wants a scan. It happens,' she added, when Samantha said it was a shame. 'But do stay on as long as you like. I won't be able to drive you back, but reception will rustle up a taxi for you.'

So Samantha stayed in the pool until Kate, Farida and Max left, and she played with the Persian family until their father decided it was time for them all to get out and have tea.

Peace. What bliss! Samantha floated on her back, blinking up at the sky, noticing the sun was already beginning to go down as the mid-afternoon shadows slanted towards the edge of the pool. It wasn't so hot now—or was she getting used to it? She rolled over in the water a couple of times, then floated again, her reverie punctuated by the cries from the minaret as the Muslims began their ritual prayers. She smiled contentedly. This was really Arabia—a fascinating land of contrasts . . .

Suddenly someone dived into the water, sending rocky, disturbing waves to wash her under. She looked round quickly—the children perhaps?—or their father? But the figure breaking surface, treading water and flicking the hair out of eyes, was Max Kramer.

He smiled at her, then was gone again, darting out of sight, and she kicked out, hating the idea of him swimming around her legs. He came crashing up to the surface again, this time close behind her, and she started swimming for the side; there was no way she was staying out of her depth with that man around!

'Running away?' he taunted, long, powerful strokes letting him easily catch her.

She clutched at the handrail and glared at him. 'I thought you'd gone.'

'Many talents I may have,' he said, watching the water trickle off her face, down her neck . . . between her breasts, 'but brain surgery isn't one of them.' If it was meant to be a joke, Samantha didn't laugh. 'Look,' he tried again, his voice and eyes serious, 'about last night . . .'

'There's nothing to say about last night. Forget it.'

He touched her arm without thinking. 'Perhaps I can help . . .'

'Help? *You?*' Samantha laughed in his face; if she hadn't she would have cried. 'I've met men who thought they could help. Let's say the cure was worse than the disease, and leave it at that.' She dived away from him, not really sure in which direction she was heading. As he caught up with her and she put her foot down for support, it was a bit of shock to discover that she was way out of her depth.

'Bad as that?' he asked, and the deep controlled voice was icy—wary.

'It's none of your business.'

'Maybe I'm making it my business.'

'You don't have the right.' She was treading water furiously, trying to keep upright. He was between her and the handrail . . .

'I didn't meant to make you ill . . .' he said, suddenly realising she was getting tired, and supporting her elbows with his hands. On the terrace Samantha could see the Persian family making tracks to leave. There were only a couple of other people in the shallow end, even the pool attendant seemed engrossed in a paperback over in the corner. 'You must have had a very rough time,' he added softly, and his eyes were all over her again and she felt the pounding begin as their legs twisted together.

His limbs felt smooth, hard, the silky soft skin covering powerful muscles. She had thought Kate's Persian friend had been a well-made man, but Max Kramer's male strength was emphasized by an almost tangible sensuality. He seemed to be aware of her femininity right down to her fingertips. Yes, he liked women, in his own chauvinistic way. Sue-Lee, Jessica, Farida; three more diverse women she couldn't imagine. But he was wasting his time with Samantha. In fact, why was he bothering at all? Only the other day he had made it perfectly clear that she ought to return to the U.K. . . . But she watched as swimming pool waves splashed against his broad chest, the smattering of auburn hair tangling into wet curls.

'You didn't make me ill,' she said at last, because suddenly it was important that he shouldn't believe he had that much effect on her. But her fascinated stare continued as his well-manicured hands stroked the water, helping to keep them both afloat. He wasn't wearing a ring . . . 'I told you last night,' she battled on 'it's nothing personal. I just don't happen to think much of men.'

Brown eyes reflected the sun bouncing back from the water. Everything seemed very quiet—very deserted. 'I think you're mistaken.' He had the nerve to reach out and touch the shoulder strap of her tiny black bikini. 'Very fetching. You like to be noticed, Samantha. And when I arrived you didn't seem to mind playing the fool with Hassan.' His eyes darkened. 'In fact, you seemed to be enjoying it.'

'Don't judge everyone by yourself,' she said, trying to break away, but he pulled her back, demanding an explanation, and she added, 'I was only having an innocent game; his *wife* was in the pool, for heaven's sake! But I wouldn't expect someone like you to understand the meaning of innocence,' she finished angrily, having a sudden vision of the young Sue-Lee.

'There was nothing innocent in that horseplay. I saw his eyes—I saw *your* eyes . . .'

'Jealous?' she challenged, without daring to consider the outcome, and to her horror Max grabbed both her shoulders and stared down at her, a strange, unknown expression on his face.

'Jealous?' he repeated, and there was a husky, seductive growl behind the word. Then his eyes lowered to her mouth, her chin . . . down to that taunting cleavage once again, and beyond, to the distorted shape of her body beneath the water. 'You, know—you could be right,' he said, looking into her startled green eyes again. 'Maybe I am jealous. But one thing's certain; you're a very mixed up lady. You may have problems—but I don't think hating me is one of them.' And before she could even begin to wonder what he meant by that, he was drawing her nearer, until their bodies met—and then their lips.

As Samantha began to struggle they both disappeared beneath the water . . .

CHAPTER FIVE

DOWN, down, in a slow balletic spiral, Max's arms firm about her, his strong lethal body embracing her own. Panic stilled as Samantha clutched his shoulders, instinct telling her that he was hardly likely to let either of them drown.

The kiss went on and on, the water cradling them in its warm sensuousness ... Now he was coiling a leg around one of hers ... drawing her even closer ... Excitement and anger kicked in her stomach—how *dared* he! She began struggling again, feeling suddenly short of breath ... But their descent had stopped, in fact, they were already going up, and suddenly they had broken surface, and broken the kiss, but Max was still holding her, shaking the water from his eyes; eyes whose wickedness taunted her.

She hit him. The sound echoed round the swimming pool and someone down the other end laughed.

'Ten out of ten for muscle power,' she said angrily. 'Is that how you get your kicks? Women and children who haven't the strength to fight back? I told you I didn't have much of an opinion of men, Mr Kramer, and your behaviour only confirms my theory!' Actually she would have liked to scream that he was a chauvinistic pig and could go to hell, but she wasn't giving him the satisfaction of completely losing her self-control. 'Now, take your hands off me!' Her voice rose in tight anger and he instantly released her, but the taunting, menacing smile never left his face.

'Come on, Sam, don't pretend you didn't enjoy it.'

'My name is *Samantha*—and if you think I enjoyed . . .'

'Have dinner with me tonight,' he persisted.

'Go to hell!' She swam to the side and climbed out, but he was beside her as she reached the table and chairs. She grabbed a towel, covering herself, reaching for the bag and sunglasses . . .

'Who was he?' Max Kramer's voice was strangely still.

'Who was who?' she asked, pretending not to understand.

'The fellow who's given you this chip on your shoulder. Let you down, did he? Honey, we've all had love affairs that went wrong. You can't spend the rest of your life blaming the opposite sex. Besides,' he added, those brown eyes dark and taunting again, 'just think of the waste.' And his subtle gaze was filled with every line and curve of her visible below the short towel. 'Is that why you try to do a man's job?' he continued, more seriously. 'Are you trying to pay him back? Prove something?'

'That's just the kind of remark I'd expect from you,' she grated. 'Why does anything have to be a *man's* job? I like my work and I'm as capable as anyone of doing it. And I've no quarrel with a *love* affair that doesn't work out,' she added quickly, emphasising a word of which he had probably no conception. 'My objection is with men who believe they're irresistible— and are prepared to prove the point by physical force if necessary.'

'You're not suggesting—back there . . .' He pointed towards the pool, cross, serious, half laughing at the idea.

'I'm not *suggesting* anything, Mr Kramer. I'm *telling* you. I've met your sort before, and they make me sick!'

'But you weren't, were you?—this time,' he said,

and she frowned in confusion. 'You weren't sick,' and when she still didn't seem to know what he was saying, he added harshly, 'My physical presence didn't make you throw up.'

Green eyes stared at him with a mixture of surprise and horror. 'I told you I can take care of myself,' she said, recovering quickly. But as she marched into the changing room and stood under the shower, she felt breathless—pleased with herself. Had she broken the curse—was she on the way to a cure?

Max Kramer was waiting for her when she went down to reception. 'Kate said you didn't have your car,' he began, getting up from one of the low chairs and strolling across to her. He looked very tall, very masculine, in minuscule white shorts and sports shirt. Lord, he did have incredible legs ... 'I can give you a lift,' he added, perfectly aware of her assessment, his experience telling him when a woman was interested.

Samantha felt her face go tight. Why did she always feel so physically aware of him? 'No, thanks,' she said. 'I'll get a taxi.'

He glanced at the vacant reception desk. 'Everyone seems to have disappeared.' Was it a coincidence—or had it cost him?

'I'll wait,' she glared.

'Look, I'm going your way. Don't be ridiculous. I only have to pick up Lee first.'

'Oh—your *ward*,' said Samantha, without attempting to hide her sarcasm.

'Yes, my ward.' His lips thinned as she gave a disbelieving little laugh. 'And what's that supposed to mean?' The old aggression licked across his face.

'Why should it mean anything?' she said sweetly.

'I am Lee's guardian.' He knew what she was getting at all right.

'You don't have to explain to me,' she taunted.

'Your affairs are your own business, Mr Kramer.' But that seemed to be going just a little too far.

'Sue-Lee is fifteen years old,' he hissed quietly, yet his voice and eyes were filled with contempt. 'Her father was a friend of mine. He is now dead. She is living with me for the time being—and when I say *living*, I mean sharing my home.' He spoke with exaggerated preciseness. 'Is that clear, Miss Whittaker? If you spread any other story, I warn you, I shall sue. Now, do you want that lift or not?'

'I thought you always left with the lady you came in with,' she taunted, so as not to show that his threat had shaken her.

'It doesn't apply when the lady deserts me first.' There was a touch of reluctant humour acknowledging her sharp quip. Once again their mutual antipathy was peppered with a deep, mutual fascination.

'All right, you can give me a lift,' said Samantha, without really knowing where the words came from, and Max led the way out into the heat again, and towards a long, low, black American car.

'You went out to the rig this morning?' he asked, when they were slowly wending their way towards the main road. Samantha was still groping for her sunglasses; even with tinted windows it was still pretty bright. 'Are they still up to schedule?' he added.

'Of course.'

'No problems?' He glanced at her sideways before swinging out on to the main road. For a moment her heart missed a beat; she still wasn't used to driving on the 'wrong' side of the road.

'Should there be any problems? Are you a born pessimist?' she asked. 'Or do you just think that because I'm in charge . . .?'

'Let's just say I've worked for Mepco before,' he interrupted.

'If you're suggesting . . .'

'I'm only suggesting that things are never the same in reality as they are at a college desk. Things go wrong. Adjustments have to be made...'

'I don't need you to tell me my job,' she snapped. 'And I'm not fresh from university, Mr Kramer. I have had several years' experience.'

His mouth twitched. 'Yeah,' he drawled, 'so you keep telling me.' But that sort of remark didn't deserve an answer, so Samantha set her face and kept staring out of the windscreen.

After a mile or so he coasted into the side of the road, near several rather smart houses, one of which appeared to be a school. 'Come on, Samantha,' he coaxed, those brown eyes watchful, a gentle finger lightly touching her shoulder. 'Why don't you have dinner with me? There's no real need for us to be bad friends. In fact, with a little good will I'm sure we could become...'

'I'm not interested in becoming anything to you, Mr Kramer.' Green eyes glared at him, but he only laughed.

'You really must call me Max.' His hand sneaked around her neck; she felt trapped in her seatbelt, noticing that he had slipped out of his. 'It really is quite silly to fight it,' he went on calmly. 'I realise you've had it rough—but it won't always be like that. I promise you...' As he spoke he was edging closer, his face coming towards her, his dark eyes mesmerising, his lips holding a fatal fascination as he drew nearer ... nearer ...

'I don't—want—you,' she struggled to say, but the words came slowly, stilted, and she was breathless in between.

'Let's just take it one kiss at a time,' he whispered, and his breath was warm on her face now, his eyes liquid sensuality, his nearness making the little hairs on her cheek stand on end.

Samantha swallowed, as a dull, heavy throb began beating time with her heart.

'I don't—want,' she tried again . . . He wasn't touching her. The hand behind her neck had disappeared moments ago, it was probably on the back of her seat. And now Max was undoing her seatbelt with his other hand, and his arm brushed against her leg, causing a leaping excitement deep inside. This was crazy . . .

'I'm not going to hurt you,' he whispered again. 'It's still light. Lee will be coming out in a moment.' He made an exaggerated movement of keeping his hands well away.

'This is silly,' Samantha muttered, her body soft and acquiescent—waiting for him.

'Mmm—silly,' he muttered, and now at last his lips touched, and it was deep, liquid fire, burning—dissolving . . . She could taste him, smell the fresh tang of the swimming pool still lingering about him, yet beneath there was the subtle, musky fragrance of an exciting man. For a moment she gave herself up to the shock of unexpected enjoyment, and at last, overwhelming fascination made her return the kiss . . . But the moment she did so he stopped, pulling away easily and gazing down at her with those long-lashed, taunting brown eyes. 'See how nice it can be when you don't fight me,' he murmured, and now he let the tip of his index finger gently smooth her cheek.

Samantha stared at him in green-eyed wonder. It was a bit difficult thinking, and yet somehow she forced her face to remain emotionless while her brain struggled with ideas. She hadn't frozen. She hadn't felt sick—or trapped. She hadn't felt threatened. And yet wasn't that the greatest threat of all?

The pulsating silence in the car continued as Max studied her slowly and carefully, his glance travelling over her features, down her neck—across her bare arms and shoulders. She could tell he liked her light, strappy sundress and all the provocative parts of her that it displayed. Now he was picking up one of her hands, smoothing the fingers, caressing her palm. His eyes were lowered, absorbed in his simple pleasure . . .

She blinked and tried to swallow, but there was a great tide of emotion and longing . . . She wanted to reach out and return the caress. She wanted to be kissed again. 'See how nice it can be when you don't fight me,' Max's words sang round in her brain. 'Don't fight him . . . don't fight him.' And oh, how easy it would be . . . But somehow she managed to push the idea away, because common sense told her she wasn't prepared to accept the terms of such compliance. Max Kramer might be fascinated with her as a woman, maybe as a confessed man-hater she even represented an interesting challenge, but she knew his interest didn't go beyond his image of her as an attractive proposition. How could he, when he had already made clear his disapproval of her chosen career? And suddenly she could see way, way ahead down a long tunnel of a possible future—a future which included Max—where he would persuade her to give up her work and live with him.

Now he was taking her hand to his lips, smiling at her, the strong suntanned face and sensuous eyes marked with the knowledge and promise of an experienced man. She saw the edges of his lips move, the way the tousled auburn hair curled just above his collar, the smooth, firm neck and throat—the way he moved imperceptibly nearer . . . the mixture of latent sexuality, pleasure and dangerous love evident in the offering in his eyes. Oh, how easy it would be to give up everything. But how long would it last? And what about her own self-esteem?

Max began kissing her again, his hand on her bare shoulder this time, and now sliding down her arm. And her body reacted like quicksilver, a sharp, erotic knife of desire slicing her in two. And she was suddenly angry at her own physical betrayal; angry that this wretched man should have such control over her senses; angry that she didn't have more control over her own.

She broke the kiss, pushing him away. 'I think that's enough,' she said, groping for her bag of wet swimming things, then trying to find the door catch with a hand that was beginning to tremble.

'I don't think that's anywhere near enough,' he replied lightly, but his eyes were cautious, watchful—little muscles jerked in his cheek as he tried to assess her sudden change of mood. Was he afraid she was going to be sick all over his car? Then her heightened colour seemed to reassure him. 'What's the matter, Sam?' he asked quietly, and the unexpected softness behind the words brought a sudden lump to her throat. She had to get out of here—fast. 'I'm not going to touch you,' he said, as she kept struggling with the door catch. 'Lee will be here in a minute.' But it was no good, she couldn't bear him being near her. There was something there, behind his eyes—something that touched her secret, vulnerable soul.

'I'm going to get a taxi,' she said, scrambling out of the car at last, and slamming the door shut before he could stop her.

'Samantha!'

She heard him open his door, begin to climb out, and she was looking about wildly for a taxi, willing one to come along. And then there were two competing for her custom, the first one reached her by executing a swift U-turn and sliding up to her in a shower of dust, and without bothering to worry what the rest of his driving was like, Samantha piled into the back and gave him her address.

As the taxi streaked away, she turned round and

stared out of the back window, in time to see Max Kramer slamming his car door in rage and giving one of his tyres a kick. Before a large truck obscured her view she thought she saw Sue-Lee running up to him . . .

She settled back in her seat, breathing more easily now—certain that Max wouldn't try to follow her. Her curls were blowing all over the place. The old taxi had no air-conditioning, so the windows were wound right down, and as they tore along without regard for speed limit, the wind felt as if it was coming from a giant hair-dryer . . . At this rate she would be home in five minutes.

As she began fishing for her purse, she remembered the glimpse of Sue-Lee, or Lee, as Max had called her. Strange, but somehow she had believed him when he had insisted that he was no more than the young girl's guardian. The more she was getting to know Max Kramer, the more she was realising that he would be interested in women as experienced as himself. No, there was no reason for her to be jealous of Lee.

Jealous? But I'm not—not at all, she thought quickly. I don't *care* about Max. He's dangerous— deadly. But didn't he constitute an even greater danger for the simple reason that she could so easily begin to care? Samantha gave herself a mental shake as she directed the driver to her particular bungalow. She was mad to consider Max Kramer in any relationship other than the purely professional. But as she spent a weary evening cooking supper and watching a video movie, she found that it wasn't easy to shut the man completely out of her mind.

Eventually she slipped into bed, lying naked between the cool sheets, her exhausted body sighing after its long day. But her mind was still wide awake, returning to the discussion out at the rig and the possible danger of pulling 'wet strings'. And what would Max have to say to that? She tossed about a bit and thumped her pillow. But then it was another Max pictured on the darkened ceiling, and this Max was smiling at her, those brown eyes taunting, a hand stretched towards her, and it was so tempting—so tempting... And then she was cross with him for taking advantage of her in the pool, and for daring to kiss her again in the car. And he had been right; she hadn't felt sick—and there had been none of that dreadful hysteria.

And yet was that so very surprising? She had grown up a normal, healthy girl, enjoying the company of men, falling in love—getting engaged. And although, in retrospect, perhaps breaking up had been the best thing all round, it hadn't felt like it at the time. She had been deeply hurt, yet—well, there had never been that abandonment with Bob. She had always found it easy to hold back. She had never slept with him. And if she had really been in love with him, would such restraint have been that easy? If she was engaged to Max Kramer would she be able to stop him—or rather, would she be able to stop herself?

Angry at such thoughts, Samantha thumped her pillow again and tossed the spare one on the floor. Yet her broken engagement hadn't turned her off men as a sex. That had only happened with that dreadful man in the car... She shut her mind to all that. So if she hadn't felt sick this afternoon in the pool, or with Max in his car, it only meant that he had tapped back to her old self—her old loving, trusting self. That vulnerable spot that she didn't want to think about these days.

Yet where did all that leave her? Free, now, to develop a relationship with any new man? Or trapped in Max Kramer's stormy whirlwind of desire?

She eventually drifted off into a troubled, restless sleep peppered with dreams, not of the man in the car, but of being in the middle of a tug-of-war. When the alarm went off she was still so tired she felt like hurling the clock against the wall. But maybe there was some good in the day, and staggering out into the kitchen she suddenly realised with relief that she wouldn't have to see Max Kramer for three whole days. And there couldn't be much better news than that!

'A *wet string*! You're telling me you want to pull a wet string?' Three days had flown; Frank's little office out at the rig vibrated as Max Kramer's fist came down on the table. 'I knew it!' He exchanged glances with his assistant, a tough man in his forties, with an international accent that could have come from anywhere. It was he who would be in charge of the drill stem testing next week. As head of Gulf Services, Max's presence in these preliminary discussions was purely formal. Now there was a sharpness in his eyes as the two men silently acknowledged some secret, prearranged decision. 'I take it you're trying to save rig time—and therefore your money,' he continued to Frank and Samantha saw the older man flush with rage.

'There are other reasons,' she broke in, 'not that there's anything wrong with saving money. We want a good sample, Mr Kramer, we don't want it contaminated, neither do we want it washed away with mud.'

'You don't have to explain to me,' he snapped, shuffling papers in front of him, glancing down at his report. 'But if there's a build-up of gas, if anything goes wrong . . .'

'Are you suggesting my crew can't cope?' This was the tool pusher, the big American in charge of the drilling floor. 'We haven't had a blow-out in all my thirty years . . .'

'Then good for you,' said Max.

The argument went on and on; Frank became more

and more red and the tool pusher was an aggressive as
Max, his fist bigger if anything, his language modified
with difficulty because Samantha was present.

'You've already decided, haven't you?' Max stared
at Frank, knowing that, as company man, he had the
last say on anything that happened out here.

'Yeh, we've already decided,' Frank confirmed, his
eyes flashing angrily behind his steel-rimmed glasses.

'Regardless of the consequences?' Max stared hard
at Samantha as he spoke.

'If you don't like the heat you should stay out of the
kitchen,' she said. Out of the corner of her eye she saw
Frank grin, but Max's eyes were cold and hard—his
face grim.

'Right!' He glanced at his assistant. 'Then *I'll* do
this job. You can go over to Kuwait next week,' and it
was pretty clear that he had arranged all this in case
anything unexpected should happen here.

'Aren't you rather overreacting?' said Samantha,
knowing she had Frank and the tool pusher on her
side.

'I said I'm taking over!' He glared at Frank as he
spoke and the two men locked into a fierce eye battle.
'I'm not having any of my men taking unnecessary
risks . . .' He broke off, obviously having plenty more
to say, but not wishing to do so in public. 'Like I
said,' this time he glared at Samantha, 'I've worked
for this company before.'

What was that supposed to mean? But before she
could think of a suitably cutting reply, Max had
expressed a desire to go up on the rig, and everyone
went off with him, except Samantha and Frank, who
was pacing over to his desk, pulling open a drawer and
reaching for a box of cigars.

'A little of that guy goes a long way,' he said, biting
the end off the cigar and spitting it into the waste bin.
Samantha's eyes widened, she had never seen anyone

actually do that before! 'Still thinking you're going to like this job?' he demanded harshly, anger making him break two matches before the huge Havana was lit.

'Max Kramer won't make any difference to my opinion of this or any job,' she said firmly, and the words somehow brought to a conclusion all the uncertainties of the past few days. *If* Max Kramer was interested in her as a woman, and *if* she wanted to develop the relationship, he would have to come to terms with her career—but after the heat and tension of this office during the past hour, she didn't think that either eventuality was very likely.

'I've got one or two things to check in my office,' she said, leaving Frank to his cigar. He seemed about to stop her going, then changed his mind and dismissed her with a disgruntled wave of his hand.

As she crossed the hot, dusty track to another Portakabin, Samantha wondered just what had happened in the past between Kramer and Frank. Why did Max feel it essential to supervise the drill stem testing just because they were going to pull a wet string? But as she reached her office she shrugged the question aside. Perhaps with a man like Max there weren't any straight answers, and she realised that beneath the tall, tough, intelligent exterior there lay the subtle conflictions of a very complex man.

On her first visit out to the rig, she had found only one hat and the giant rubberised slickers in her cupboard, and Frank had asked someone to get a smaller set from stores. She just wanted to check up that they had arrived ... Yes, they had—then something on the new hard hat, high up on the shelf, suddenly caught her eye.

She pulled it down, laughing, turning it over in her hands. It was a very nice new shining yellow hat. She plonked it on after adjusting it much smaller. But the devils had decorated the crown with several stickers, the sort of cheeky things the men stuck on their own hats. One of hers said 'Red', another 'Ginger'— referring to her red curls, of course. But the sauciest one was centre front, a punched-out tape which read— HOT LIPS! After one visit the men had already decided what to call her. Samantha grinned, knowing it could have been a lot worse—experience telling her that the nickname would stick.

She put the hat back and pulled out the slickers. Good, they looked more her size, although she hoped she would never have to wear them; there were going to be no mistakes, no accidents for her to need protective clothing on *her* rig. Samantha suddenly felt proud of the faith the company had in her experience and skills. She knew this job was right for her. She had a lot to learn, but already she was a good engineer.

Frank was still alone when she went back into his office, and he actually laughed when she told him about the hat. Someone had brought in coffee, and he poured her a mug, muttering about how long Kramer would be, because he had a heavy evening of meetings and wanted to get back to Dubai.

Samantha perched on the edge of his desk, sipping her coffee, deciding she ought to go out and start talking to the men, get to know them, get the feel of the place . . . But then she realised that Frank had finished on the radio telephone and was talking to her. There were voices from outside as well; she wondered if Max was coming back . . .

'Have you been getting about?' Frank was asking now, and Samantha stopped thinking about Max. 'Joined any clubs—are you making plenty of friends?' His smile twisted as he half-joked, 'I wouldn't like to think of you sitting home alone at nights!'

She laughed back, not sure of his mood, wondering whether the lonely nights really referred to himself, and whether he was making her some sort of opening

to talk about his wife. 'I thought I might join the local
Morris Dancing team,' she said, still unsure about
invading his privacy. 'They actually allow *women* to
dance with them—very liberated!' Then she shrugged.
'But I haven't got round to doing it yet—not sure if
I'll have the energy to go leaping around with them
after one of Mepco's normal working days!'

'Sounds far too energetic,' he agreed. 'What you
need is a cabaret and meal. What do you say, Sam?'
He came round his desk, she was still perched on the
edge, and it took a big effort not to step away. 'I've got
some tickets for tomorrow night at the Sheraton.
Would you like to come?' and as he put an arm
around her shoulders, the old panic flared and she
jumped, dropping the mug, spilling hot coffee over
them both.

'Oh, what a fool thing to do!' She grabbed a handful
of tissues from the box on his desk. 'It just slipped—
are you hurt?'

'It only got my shoes.' He didn't seem to suspect
anything, but as she dabbed at her cotton trousers,
Samantha was horrified to see that her hand was
shaking. Surely she hadn't been really scared? 'So
are you?' Frank persisted, 'free tomorrow night?' and
before she could think what to say, they both became
aware of someone standing in the doorway.

'No, she isn't free tomorrow night.' It was Max.
How long had he been there? What had he seen? 'She
already has a date with me. Isn't that so, darling?'

She looked straight into his eyes and her stomach
flipped over. Oh, he was clever, his manner
proprietorial enough to hint at a personal relationship,
yet his anger limited because he knew Frank could be
no real rival.

'I—yes, I'm afraid I'm already booked up,' she
stammered to Frank. She didn't like lying; lies had a
habit of bouncing back.

He didn't seem upset, but shrugged and straightaway asked Max something about the well, so Samantha escaped and made her way to the canteen, determined not to get involved in whatever feud was brewing between the two men.

Lunch wasn't quite ready, the canteen was practically empty, so she took her replacement cup of coffee to a corner table and sat brooding in brief solitude.

Fool! Why let Max Kramer get you out of trouble? Now he'll think you can't look after yourself. Maybe he'll even think you fancy him. You could have handled Frank. He's harmless enough . . . Just a lonely man missing his wife. It wouldn't even have hurt you to have dinner with him. You could have been a bit of company . . . But she hadn't accepted his invitation because the old fear had been there, and when that happened she couldn't think straight. Yet she mustn't let Max think he had won. But how? Maybe she would think of something while she was driving back to town. But when the time came to leave, the devil was playing tricks.

'Damn!' Samantha turned the ignition again and her car gave a horrible grinding sort of noise; it was perfectly obvious that it had made up its mind not to start. 'But it's only just come back from a big garage job!' she wailed to one of the mechanics who strolled up to help.

'Have any problems on the way here?' he asked, opening the bonnet and delving inside.

'Not that I noticed.' Yet thinking back, it had seemed a bit sluggish. But this was the first time she had driven out to the rig on her own, and her concentration had been on the route and actually *getting* here.

'Trouble?' queried Frank, coming out of his office, followed by Max.

Samantha shrugged. 'It'll be all right, I expect. Can't be anything drastic—I mean, it's just been overhauled.'

'Want me to wait for you?' he asked, 'just in case?' but the pleasant gesture missed out as he glanced impatiently at his watch.

'No, go on back. I know you're in a rush.' Max was watching her and no way was she going to play the damsel in distress. As the mechanic tried to start the car again, a gust of wind blew sand into her face. 'I think I'll just go and wait in my office, if you don't mind,' she added, walking away without looking at Max again. Now perhaps he would begin to believe that she could look after herself!

She worked on for a while, then decided to make a list of the things she would have to bring out with her for an overnight stay. Next week's testing operation would go on for several days.

After a while she was about to go and find out how her car was doing when there was a knock on the door, and for some reason, instead of calling, 'Come in,' she went over and opened it herself.

A hot wind blew in her face, but she hardly noticed it. 'What the hell are you doing here?' she demanded. At the bottom of the steps Max Kramer was staring up at her.

'It's time we were leaving,' he said. 'I don't like the look of the weather.' And then, more angrily, 'Your car is out of commission—it needs a spare part—something that should have been replaced after its accident, but wasn't. You're lucky it got you this far.' And when she obviously didn't believe him, he added, 'Make up your own mind—but I'm leaving now.'

'Why did you stay behind?' Oh no, this was too much!

'Frank wanted to get back to town, remember? and *someone* had to make sure you weren't stranded.'

He looked tall and dangerous, in cream trousers and bush-style shirt creased and crumpled now, his hair dishevelled from the hot wind outside, his face deeply bronzed with little pale creases in the corners of his eyes where he had screwed them up against the sun. His desert boots were dusty; only the slim, expensive watch on his wrist spoke of that other, luxurious side of the oil business, and Samantha suddenly remembered the Hilton restaurant in Al Ain on the day of the camel market. There she had seen the subtle glimpses of immense wealth displayed by Middle Eastern businessmen.

But this wasn't the Hilton, and they weren't surrounded by even the surface glamour of sophistication. This was the desert, and thirty miles lay between her and the refuge of cosmopolitan Dubai. Thirty miles didn't sound far—but in the desert it was an awfully long way.

She continued staring at him, her heart racing in growing horror because the prospect of such a journey—with only Max Kramer for company—suddenly appeared to be infinitely exciting!

CHAPTER SIX

'You drive,' taunted Max, as Samantha was about to climb into the Range Rover. 'Let me see how your sand driving has improved.'

Improved! It was pretty obvious he was expecting her to make a fool of herself, and she was about to argue, but then saw a couple of men strolling over to say goodbye, and somehow she didn't want to demonstrate her anger with Max in public. 'I know you don't think very much of my driving,' she said, climbing into the driving seat and wincing as she kangarooed a couple of times; naturally a big thing like this took a bit of getting used to. Max made an exaggerated grab for the handrail on the dash in front of him. She ignored it, and waved goodbye, laughing at the cheeky remarks thrown up to the departing Hot Lips, trying at the same time to find the gear lever.

'Here.' Max caught her hand and guided it to the gear-stick. Now, why was he angry?

She snatched her hand away and changed gear. The vehicle lurched again and she cursed under her breath. Slowly, getting the feel of the thing at last, they left the large, levelled-out area of the rig, and she cautiously followed the beaten track down between small, scrappy sand-dunes. Max had been right, the wind was getting quite bad. From time to time a sudden gust would send a shower of stinging hot sand against the windscreen. But she persevered in silence for at least half an hour, aware of the man sitting sideways next to her, his continued silence eloquently hostile.

'Is this as fast as you intend to go?' he asked at last, glancing at his watch. His profile was stern and unyielding as she glanced quickly at him. 'I would like to get home before dark.'

'As a matter of fact, so would I.' Why did he want to get home before dark? she added to herself. Did he have a date?

There was silence again as she negotiated a rough stretch where loose sand had blown over the track. They had just passed one of the red-painted oil-drums that marked their route. Now she strained ahead for the next one—yes, there it was.

'How far do you think you'll be able to see in the dark?' Max could contain himself no longer. She had been aware of him breathing heavily, as if forcing himself to remain calm, for at least ten minutes. 'We're a bit short on street lights out here, as you've probably noticed.'

'Funny!' She glared at him quickly. 'What you really mean is, you don't think I'm capable of getting us out of here.'

'You possibly could. Given time—which,' he reminded her, glancing at his watch, 'is becoming preciously slim.'

'It's barely four o'clock—we've got a good two hours . . .' But she broke off because he wasn't listening, but was looking out of his window, looking behind them; almost as if he expected something to come out of the sky.

'Let me drive,' he said.

'Changing your mind? Scared of lady drivers, are you?'

'Samantha . . .'

'Don't you "*Samantha*" me!' She was aware of the tension coiling in them both, but she didn't have time for conversation, because they were passing between some high, curly dunes and the wind was whipping the sand off the tops, making the visibility momentarily hazy.

She changed down and was only doing twenty again. Let him complain—go on, just let him complain, but the track was a bit difficult to see and quite narrow here. The edges looked pretty soft; was it possible for even a four-wheel-drive truck to get stuck in that lot? But in a minute they would be through this patch and the going would be flatter—if she remembered correctly.

Then suddenly, out of the corner of her eye, she saw a camel nosing at a scrappy bush, and then another one . . . She smiled to herself, wanting to remember this moment; real camels in the real desert . . . The track did a sharp turn around a big dune, Samantha was still dreaming about the camels, when suddenly there was a whole bunch of the creatures ambling slowly across her path as if they were out on a Sunday afternoon stroll.

'Look out!' Max grabbed his handrail, bracing himself for the impact, but Samantha had no intention of hitting any of them. She slammed on the brake and spun the wheel her way—the back skidded, a few camels actually broke into a trot . . . and then the Range Rover left the track and came to a stop down the bottom of a little slope, only unfortunately it was tilted at a bit of a funny angle.

Good! They hadn't hit any of the camels. 'Stupid creatures!' she shouted back at them. 'Didn't you hear me coming?'

'*They've* been coming this way for thousands of years,' Max informed her tightly. 'Maybe they thought you ought to give way.'

'Thousands of years! Really?' Samantha fumed. 'Don't look that old, do they?'

'You were going too fast.' He wasn't going to let her get away with it.

'It was you who wanted to go faster!'

'Back there,' he said, 'on the open stretch, not among this lot!' He opened his door and leaned out round the back. 'Come on,' he shouted, still hanging out. 'Into reverse—*carefully!*'

Samantha gritted her teeth. If there was one thing she couldn't stand, it was men telling her how to drive. She had actually thought for herself that *reverse* might be the best idea; the alternative was a forty-five-degree climb straight up a dune.

'Carefully!' Max shouted again, as the Range Rover began nudging its way backwards up the slope. 'That's it, nearly there . . .' Only she was being so delicate that there wasn't quite enough power . . . a bit more—a bit. But her stupid foot slipped down on the accelerator, the back wheels spun and she felt them dig down into the sand. Oh no!

'I *said*—carefully.' Max flung himself back into the cab.

'How do you expect me to concentrate if you keep shouting?' she screamed back, switching off the engine and climbing down to go and have a look herself. Wind whipped the door out of her hand and it banged against the side of the truck. Sand stung her face and she had to screw up her eyes as she battled her way round to the rear. The camels had gone, of course. There was nothing but the wind, the desert, the stranded car—and Max Kramer.

'I'll get the planks and the shovels,' he said icily, and she ought to have known that he would be prepared for anything. But as fast as they tried to dig the wheels out, the sand blew straight back, and it was getting pretty difficult even to stand up. 'Okay, that's enough—there's no point carrying on.' Max threw his shovel back inside and Samantha could see that to dig any more would be quite useless.

'But what can we *do*?' she demanded, climbing back

inside and trying to brush the sand out of her hair. 'How long will it go on?'

He shrugged. 'Maybe minutes, maybe an hour—maybe longer. Never can tell with a sandstorm.'

'*Sandstorm?*' Stupidly, the idea hadn't occurred to her. 'But we could be stuck here for . . .?'

'Precisely.' Now there was no point in controlling his anger, he let her have it full blast. 'And I suppose you realise that the others are probably back in Dubai now. Where we should have been. I told you women are dangerous in this business.'

'Oh yes,' she snapped, furious with the great giant of a man whose dominant force of will overpowered the cab. 'A sandstorm's quite easy to organise—you want to see what I can arrange when I'm really trying!'

'Don't be stupid!'

'Stupid? If you think I'm responsible for this,' she said sarcastically, gesticulating out of the window, 'then you're the one who's stupid!' And there was something growing between them, something that brought a dangerous light to his eyes, something that made her breathing quicken. 'Anyway,' she continued, 'I don't know what *you've* got to be angry about. *I* didn't ask you to stay behind. I could have got a lift—or borrowed a truck,' and something told her she was far too near the truth for his comfort. 'So why not just—leave me to it?' she taunted.

'Because——' he seemed to be groping for an answer, 'because I've already told you, the desert is no place for a lady. Both of us are stuck here, which is maybe—I said, *maybe*—one degree better than you being stuck here alone. Nothing to say?' Now it was his turn to taunt, as she glared out of the windscreen. 'Good. Then perhaps you'll take my advice and go back home where you belong. *When* I've managed to get us both out of here.' She thought he had finished as he bounced back in his seat and raked unsteady hands through his sandy hair. But it was all still charging round in his mind, he was still furious and frustrated at being caught out here in this windblown turmoil. 'You women want equality,' he grated after a moment, and she could tell he was stretched just about as far as he could go without breaking, 'but the dangerous thing is—you haven't yet learned how to handle it!'

'Equality?' she screamed at last, now almost beside herself with rage. 'Who wants to be equal with you— you rude, arrogant, overbearing brute!' And before she knew what she was doing, and certainly before he had time to stop her, she wrenched open the driver's door and jumped down into the sand.

'Samantha!' But his voice was immediately lost in the hot, wild wind that almost blew her over, but she only stumbled, arms over her face, not caring what happened as long as she got away from him.

'Samantha . . .' This time his voice caught up with her. 'For God's sake, girl!'

Girl! She'd show him, she'd . . . but now he had caught up with her, his hand grasping her arm, the wind and sand trying to tear them apart.

'Let me go—get out of my way!' But the sand was everywhere and she had to bury her face in his shirt, and it was obvious that he couldn't see much either. They both began slithering down a steep, sandy slope . . . then they lost their footing and rolled together, over and over, Max and the sand and the wind . . . a maelstrom of hopeless confusion welding them together for all time . . . Heaven alone knew where the truck was now.

'Get back inside,' he was saying now, and apparently heaven had relinquished its secrets to Max, because he seemed to know where he was dragging her, but she didn't want to go back in there with him—she couldn't stand the sound of his accusing voice, his angry eyes. She didn't want him to hate her any more . . .

So she started to struggle again, and that only made him more angry, and now he was picking her up, struggling up the slope, wrenching open the passenger door this time, and practically hurling her inside.

'Get in there—and stay there,' he grated, slamming the door shut and battling his way round to the other side. 'Don't ever do that again!' His eyes blazed their anger. 'You could have got lost in this lot. If I hadn't found you . . .' He broke off, trying to shake the sand out of his hair, brushing the back of his neck, and he was really mad—so mad that words failed him. But it was more than that—as if he was battling with some private storm of his own. And then there was a really vicious gust, stronger than anything before; the car rocked and for a dreadful moment Samantha wondered if it would topple over.

'Scared?' he demanded. 'Because you should be!'

'How could I possibly be scared with the great Max Kramer to protect me?' she shouted back against the sound of the rising wind. Stinging grey sand was thrown up against the windows, then it swirled and howled and screeched away. But there was just as much danger shut up in here. And suddenly she remembered that first meeting in Max's office, that first time he had discovered that *Sam* Whittaker was a woman. He had kissed her, and through her fury she had heard the words, 'Supposing we're not here in some nice cosy office with a secretary within shouting distance . . . Supposing we're stuck out in the desert—in a truck—alone. Cut off.' And now the unlikely prospect had come true—and for a moment she was trapped in the crazy notion that he had planned it all, planned everything from that first business meeting—perhaps even from the very first time they had met in the camel market. But that was ridiculous—ridiculous . . .

Max's eyes were as restless as the raging sandstorm outside. He was breathing deeply, still brushing sand out of his shirt, still raking strong fingers through his sandblown hair. But all the time he was watching her; watching her green flashing eyes, her heaving chest, her expression of passionate rage and the deep, smouldering, conflicting emotions—all the things she felt for this man that couldn't be named.

'And don't think the sandstorm has reached its peak,' he said harshly. 'This is just a breeze. Maybe it'll blow over, or maybe it'll get worse. In which case we have to leave the car.'

'You're joking! There's no way I'm going out there again. Even stopping in here with you would be better than that.'

'Don't count on it.' He looked as if he was having difficulty keeping his hands off her. 'You felt the wind just now. Do you fancy being in here when the lot goes over?' At last his fingers curled around her arm. 'That's what I meant, don't you see?' he roared, giving her a shake, and there was a wildness in his eyes now, a wildness that matched the frightening storm outside. 'How do you think you'd get on alone? You're not only a danger to others—you're a danger to yourself as well!'

Samantha tried to hit his hand away. It was so hot—so claustrophobic in here, with the windows tight shut and no air-conditioning running. 'Why the hell should you worry what danger *I'm* in? If I'd been on my own maybe I would have driven on in the storm—lost the track—and maybe I'd have just disappeared, and then you wouldn't have had to worry about me again.'

'Of all the damn fool things to say!' Heat beat out of him, it bounced around the tiny confined space. There were damp patches on his shirt, Samantha felt a trickle of perspiration run down her own back. 'Don't you care what happens to you?' he ranted on, almost beside himself with fury, and suddenly their eyes met in a dangerous warning that mirrored anger, frustration and unbridled, mutual passion. The atmosphere was thick with a knife-edged tension.

'Max—no,' she stammered, instantly aware what was coming.

'You mean, Max—yes,' he breathed, and then he was kissing her; wild, aggressive, unrestrained kisses that fought and plundered her own dark warmth.

'You fiend,' she mumbled from a tight throat. But she didn't mean it—or only half meant it. Because this was what she wanted, this extravagance, this excitement. His hands were everywhere, sliding down her arms, her body, pulling down the zip of her yellow jump-suit, exploring the delicate lace of her bra. She was mad—mad, not to be screaming out for him to stop. Someone was moaning. At last she realised it was herself. It was a moan that came from all the unknown desires she had been holding back for so long—had *wanted* to hold back—until she had seen that tall, exciting figure striding towards her at the camel market.

Oh no, not since then! Now she began kissing him frantically, her fingers tangling in his hair, revelling in the feel of that strong, tense neck. This was madness, she tried to tell herself again, as a sharp, white-hot excitement licked inside her. How was it possible to hate someone, yet to want them desperately? And he didn't even like her. The hand caressing her breast with menacing expertise was only meant as a punishment.

And as if to emphasise the point, he was suddenly ending the kiss, pulling back from her, raking unsteady fingers through his wayward dark hair again.

'The sandstorm—it's stopping,' he said huskily, staring out of the windscreen and gripping the steering wheel until the knuckles of his suntanned hands showed through white.

Samantha took a steadying breath and pulled up her long front zip. Was that all? One passionate, devastating embrace—and then nothing. Not even 'thanks'. Boy, he was a cool customer! Didn't he feel anything? And all the while her mind was in a turmoil, remembering every time they had met—at the night club, in the swimming pool where he had kissed her, taunted her . . . Or had he only been trying to prove that he could make her want him? That she wasn't really a man-hater because with him she wouldn't feel sick or afraid? Afraid? How long ago all that seemed now. Max Kramer had taken her through the self-imposed barrier of her mind—and out towards the stars . . .

And it all meant nothing to him.

'Do you think we could open the window—just a crack?' she asked, trying to sound ever so casual, as she wiped a sleeve across her forehead. She was wringing wet—so was he.

He glanced at her sideways, then looked away quickly. 'Better wait a minute. Here, have a drink of this.' He passed her a bottle of tepid, sterile water from the emergency rations.

She drank thirstily, then passed it back to him. He only took a mouthful, and she felt guiltily extravagant, but relieved that for once he didn't complain.

They sat in silence for a while, watching the storm lose its terror, hearing the scream die to a moan. And they didn't say anything—didn't move. But the mutual battle of their minds seemed almost tangible.

'I didn't meant that to happen, back there,' Max was forced to say at last.

'I shouldn't lose any sleep over it,' Samantha answered tetchily, because it was a bit difficult controlling the pitch of her voice.

'Look, this is hardly the time or the place, is it?' he went on, and she could tell he was making a big effort to stay cool.

'The time or the place?' she repeated, not having to pretend to be confused.

He laughed harshly. 'You send out strong messages, honey.' At last he turned to look at her, his strong face unfathomable, the dark eyes strangely enigmatic. 'I wasn't expecting it—okay, the joke's on me. But at least we've got one thing sorted out. We both want each other—and the sooner the better, wouldn't you say?'

Samantha could have died of shame. Why? It was true. But was she that much of an open book? Was this the casual way he conducted all his affairs? Would he expect the same casualness from herself? She must say something quickly so that he shouldn't guess exactly how much she felt.

'I said, don't lose any sleep over it. It's purely physical, a set of chemical reactions. It doesn't mean anything.'

He gave her a long, hard look. 'My, my,' he muttered, beginning to open his door, 'a set of chemical reactions. Is that a fact?' and then he wrenched open the door viciously and was obviously about to jump down.

'Where are you going?' She was appalled at the idea of him walking out on her. Appalled that he heard the concern in her words.

'In case you hadn't noticed, the storm's more or less over. I'm going to dig us out of here.'

The sandstorm over? Never! Not this storm raging inside her—a storm swirling and revolving around her feelings for this incredible man . . . 'I'll help you,' she began.

'Stay where you are.' And she knew that really he was glad to be left on his own. Because he didn't want to be reminded of her. He didn't want to think that she had responded to his lovemaking because she actually cared. That sort of feeling wouldn't suit the cut-and-thrust world of Max Kramer. However much he might admit his physical attraction for her body, it was pretty obvious that he didn't want the complication of Samantha Whittaker in his life.

It took him half an hour to dig the wheels out, and then fifteen minutes to check the carburettor and other bits and pieces, to check that they weren't clogged with sand. At last he pronounced sentence—that they were ready to leave.

'And we'll have to get a move on,' he said, glancing at the sky and then at his watch. 'I want to get back to the main road while there's still light. It'll be impossible to follow what's left of this track when it gets dark. And I'm sure the last thing you want is to spend a night with me out here,' he added ironically.

'I do have one or two other things planned.'

'Yeah?' he drawled. 'Well, as a matter of fact, so do I.'

She taunted him with a smile. 'Got a heavy date?'

'Something like that,' was all he would say, then he started the engine, delicately inched the heavy vehicle out of the sandy dip and backed it carefully up on to the track. Damn, why couldn't she have done that earlier?

Again the silence stretched between them, as Max put his foot down and they averaged fifty once they got out on the flat. It made a pretty bumpy ride, but Samantha clutched on to the handle in front of her on the dash, and didn't complain. The last thing she wanted was to be stuck out here with Max Kramer—although she would have given anything to keep him from that date. Who was it with? She tried to imagine the elegant Syrian Farida—or was it the way-out Jessica? Or one of his other many women she hadn't even met?

At last the going was easier, they were driving among huge dunes again, but the way between them was firm and wide. It almost looked as if there hadn't been a storm at all back here. The sun was going down quickly, as it always did in the Middle East. There was going to be a good sunset over to the left, on Max's side, so she didn't choose to watch it, but instead gazed out of her own side window, as the bright blue sky lost its brilliance and made way for the passages of night.

'Wait—stop a minute, please,' she said suddenly, and Max was so surprised that he pulled up quickly in a spray of sand. Samantha wound down her window, wondering if the tinted glass was playing tricks with her eyes. But no—it was real . . . 'I won't be a minute,' she added hurriedly, jumping down and running towards the nearest dune.

She began climbing, making messy, stumbling footprints—so unlike the neat double row of camel's footprints she had once seen disappearing over a sand-dune.

At last she reached the top, and stood panting for a moment, wiping her brow with the back of her hand, revelling in the silence—in the space—in the suddenly subdued magnificence of this powerful, yet visually barren land. Beautiful, crescent-shaped dunes had curly, overhanging tops. Wind ripples had decorated them, like marks left by the receding tide. But she had seen all this before—she had stopped for another reason; a reason that even now was difficult to believe. By day the brilliant silver sun beat down on the desert sand, which reflected its rays in a glare of white heat. By day the dunes were stark, arid—nothing but windblown sand. But now, with the rapid approach of evening, it was as if the sand was soaking up the life and vigour of the setting, blood-red sun. Beneath her feet, and all around, the giant, curling dunes were taking on a new deep, rich, glowing colour—their shadow-patterns twisting and snaking, bringing a primaeval movement of their own. The dying sun seemed to give the dunes a throbbing, pulsating life. It was more than magical—it was beautiful. A wild, untamed, inexplicable beauty. So unexpected, so transient. When the sun finally set the sand would die again . . .

'Incredible, isn't it?' Max spoke softly, but she hadn't heard him coming, so his voice was a shock.

'I thought at first it was my imagination,' she said, still a bit breathless, not wanting it to end, knowing this was a little memory she would keep parcelled up and safe for all time. She was glad that, standing here now, Max would be part of that memory.

'After a while you get sort of used to it,' he said, gazing out at the desert as well. 'It's good to see it again through a newcomer's eyes . . .' and he smiled, a crooked sort of smile, and just stood there beside her. For a moment she could even pretend there was a closeness between them . . . But then the spell was broken, Max looked at his watch and said they really had to go.

It was dark a couple of miles before they reached the main road, but the track was easily distinguishable on this stretch, they could see car headlights zooming along the main road, which was a help, and the light on top of the tall Trade Centre made a comforting landmark.

It was getting on for seven when they eventually reached Mepco's office where Samantha hoped to pick up a spare car. Frank was still at his desk; didn't he ever go home?

'Say, you two look as if you've had a fight with something big!' he grinned, laughing and waving a hand towards the coffee-maker. Samantha rushed for it. She would have given a fiver for a cup of coffee a couple of hours ago.

'Actually it was a fight with a sandstorm,' said Max,

and the old hostility was back—hostility that said Frank should never have let Samantha stay on at the rig. 'It was just as well *I* waited for her,' he went on. 'We had to dig ourselves out. She couldn't have managed on her own. And whoever passed her car as mended didn't know one end of the vehicle from another. Trying to cut down on labour costs, are you?'

'I'm sure when you send in your account, we'll be paying for *your* services up to—nineteen hundred hours,' said Frank, glancing at his watch. 'Double time, is it, after six o'clock?'

Before Max could burst out with another complaint that would only have the two men standing there indefinitely, Samantha pushed a mug of coffee into Max's hand. 'Unless you'd prefer something stronger.'

His eyes swiftly covered her exhausted face. 'No, this is fine,' he said in a quieter tone. Then back to Frank again, 'Have there been any messages for me?'

Frank began searching his littered desk. Funny, but he didn't seem to be in the sort of rage she would have expected, after Max's harsh words. Perhaps they both looked such a mess that Frank considered a minor justice had been done.

'Your office phoned once or twice,' he said, 'wondering where the hell you were. And . . ' At last he found the note he was looking for, 'and some lady called half an hour ago, a Farida somebody . . .' Obviously the surname was a bit of a struggle.

'I'll phone now—may I?' Max began with firm politeness, which made Samantha sigh with relief. She really wasn't up to being in the middle of a battle between these two men. But her relief was shortlived at the sound of Farida's name. So that was his date. And he couldn't wait to phone her and make an excuse for being late.

'No,' said Frank, as Max's hand reached the phone. 'I mean, she's out, at the hospital. She phoned to cancel your date. Emergency, she said.' Frank searched his drawer for cigars. 'Nurse, is she?'

Max looked thoughtful—private. Obviously upset at their cancelled evening. 'What? Ah, no—surgeon. Ah, if you'll excuse me, I'd better be getting back. If I don't see you before, I'll pick you up around eight—tomorrow night,' he added to Samantha, and she had to give him ten out of ten for being on the ball. She had completely forgotten the bogus date they had made out at the rig, in front of Frank.

'Sure—yes,' she mumbled, trying to look nonchalant about the whole thing, when really she felt like hurling her mug of coffee in his face.

Max didn't disapprove of Farida's high-powered career, in fact the couple seemed to be very close. So where did that leave Samantha?

In a word—nowhere!

'At least we've got one thing sorted out,' he had said to her, during the sandstorm. 'We both want each other.' But wanting wasn't loving.

Did he love Farida?

CHAPTER SEVEN

'WHAT'S with the interrogation?' queried Frank, as the waiter disappeared with their lunch order. 'Out at the rig yesterday, you seemed all for pulling a wet string. Max Kramer been getting at you, has he? Is that why he offered to wait behind for you? Convincing, was he? Decided to go over to his side?'

'I didn't know we were on opposing sides,' said Samantha, sipping her cool lager and staring at the greying American. How easily the hostility built up in him when he spoke of Max. 'I've just been thinking about it, that's all.' All! She hadn't thought of anything else throughout the night!

After an exhausting day in the desert, she should have slept soundly last night. But instead she had tossed and turned, reliving the argument out at the rig. Was it safe to pull a wet string? Or was it an unnecessary risk? Round and round, the problem had refused to leave her. And when eventually she had been about to drift off to sleep, the images had changed into a sandstorm—and Max Kramer kissing her, bringing her alive—his taunting lips and intimate caresses driving her wild. There had been the mixture of Max and her need for him, the violence of the storm, and then the magical, incredible sunset when the desert had come alive . . . But it had all ended in his rejection of her—Farida's phone call cancelling their date had obviously upset him . . . But she knew she mustn't let her jealousy cloud her judgment of Max's superior experience in the oil business. And Max had made it perfectly clear that he considered the proposed operation to be highly dangerous. She had been glad, therefore, when Frank had suggested lunch today. She was pleased of the opportunity of discussing it with him again—off the record.

They had come to the International beside the creek, where she had fled for a coffee after that first meeting in Max Kramer's office. The ground floor restaurant was cool, dark and discreet, each table surrounded by high wooden partitions shaped like a dhow. There weren't many people here yet, but couples were gradually drifting in as they waited for their order.

Frank had been considering her obvious concern with the testing, and Max's opposition, and now he drained the last of his whisky in one long draught and clicked his fingers for the waiter again.

'Don't go looking for a rational explanation as far as Max Kramer is concerned,' he said sharply. 'He doesn't like Mepco—and he doesn't like me. He'd oppose whatever we suggested just for the sake of it . . .'

'Why?' Samantha interrupted. She had marked Max down for many things, but being petty wasn't one of them.

Frank twisted round, looking for the waiter, mumbling about slow service, which was a bit much. 'Why?' he repeated, turning back to her, moving knives and forks restlessly, his huge shoulders heaving in a typical shrug. 'There was an accident a couple of years ago, out on an offshore rig. A friend of his was killed . . .'

'Pulling a wet string?' she asked, with a bit of a sinking heart.

'No.' Frank attracted the waiter at last and ordered himself another drink, then went on to explain briefly the circumstances of the accident.

'But it could have happened to anyone,' said Samantha, when he had finished.

'Try telling that to Kramer. He blames Mepco—and me in particular.' He broke off as their lunch arrived; huge open sandwiches for himself and an exotic fresh fruit boat for Samantha. 'So don't let his prejudices misguide you into thinking he has all the answers.'

Samantha tentatively selected a piece of melon. 'How often has it happened? I mean, the well blowing because of pulling a wet string?'

Frank grunted his thanks as his second whisky arrived, he really seemed to be drinking an awful lot lately . . . 'Two or three times, as far as I remember,' he said at last. 'And that's after thirty years in this business, Sam. Take my advice,' he grinned, reaching across and giving her hand a pat, 'be guided by me and you won't go far wrong.'

Samantha stabbed a slice of green, glistening kiwi fruit. 'Off the record,' she began, 'is Houston really pushing for an answer?' Houston was Head Office. God. Or maybe *Mecca* would be a more appropriate term to use out here, she thought with a smile.

'Let's put it this way,' he said. 'If we don't get an answer on this well pretty soon, you and I could end up back in Houston quicker than we think.'

'At least your wife would be pleased,' Samantha was about to say, but managed to stop herself in time. Why wasn't thirty years in the field enough for Frank? Why couldn't he pack up and go home—take a desk job, and be with his family? Pressures on a man his age were dangerous . . . And more personally, she realised that she didn't want to leave Dubai—but her reasons were more tied up with people . . .

'I guess you've made me feel better,' she said instead. 'I think we both want this job over and done with as soon as possible.'

He didn't understand, or perhaps imagined she was making some reference to not wanting to lose her job. But right at this minute she was more bothered about the prospect of working in close proximity with Max next week, because some time during her restless sleep last night, Samantha had discovered that there was more than a possibility that she had fallen in love with him.

'Who are you staring at?' Frank asked after a while. 'Anyone I know?' and she only just managed to stop him turning round.

'I'm not sure,' she said, still with her mind wrapped round Max. 'A girl's just come in—I seem to recognise her—but I can't think from where.'

This time Frank was more discreet, slowly turning round and pretending to study the décor. 'Sure you do,' he said, twisting back in his seat. 'You met her at the nightclub the other evening. Friend of Kramer's—Jessica someone. Interior decorator. You remember.'

Of course! How stupid. But somehow she had forgotten about Jessica; since yesterday Farida had remained uppermost in Samantha's mind.

'Good, is she?' asked Samantha, furious to be reminded that Max should have yet another career girl in his life.

'I wouldn't know,' Frank leered. 'She's not my type.'

'You know what I mean!' Green eyes flashed a friendly warning.

'She's got her own business, if that's what you mean.' It was! 'I believe she's designed practically all the shops in the new Rashid Centre . . .'

'Really,' Samantha muttered, then managed to change the conversation on to more mundane office matters, but all the while her brain was teasing with the unfairness of it all. And how many other girl-friends did Max have with equally high-powered life-styles? Why, *why* couldn't he accept her own career in the same way?

She was still only halfway through her enormous

fruit boat when a movement over at the entrance caught her eye.

It was Max—oh no! And behind him the dark, petite figure of Sue-Lee. For a moment Samantha wanted to shrink into the shadow of her seat, to escape from the scrutiny of those dark eyes. But Max had seen her almost immediately, and then his eyes swivelled across the table to Frank, then swiftly on again, until he found Jessica, and at last he smiled, shepherding Lee in front of him as they both made their way across to the other side of the restaurant.

'Speaking of devils,' nodded Frank, belatedly noticing Max, who was, fortunately, sitting down out of Samantha's view. 'Sure you still want to keep your date with him tonight?' The alternative invitation hung heavily in his deep American burr.

'Our engagement this evening is strictly business,' she said, without a hint of a smile, and hoping that Frank wouldn't remember that Max had called her 'darling' in his office. But she would do well to forget that. To forget everything that had happened between them. They didn't really have a date—Max had just been giving her an excuse. She couldn't see him from here, but she could still see Jessica, smiling and leaning across the table, her long curls making a blonde halo against the dark wood. Max Kramer already had all he wanted. There wasn't the slightest chance that he would turn up tonight.

'What are *you* doing here?' At the stroke of eight, her bell had chimed, and as Samantha opened the front door the hot, sultry evening spilled into her cool hall. Her heart was banging wildly, even now she didn't want to acknowledge the truth. She had been so sure . . .

'I believe we have a date.' Max Kramer didn't look impressed with her simple V-necked sundress, nor with the red curls which, after a swim with Kate, had dried with more than their usual disarray. 'Or were you about to slip into something a little more elegant?' he added doubtfully. 'I've booked a table at the Hyatt Regency, then said casually, 'Do you know you can see right through that dress with the light behind it?'

Samantha practically dragged him in and slammed the door shut, before realising that that was exactly what he had intended. Of course the dress wasn't transparent. 'Our date wasn't meant to be taken seriously,' she said, trying not to notice how devastating he looked in dark trousers and white dinner jacket. The shirt looked silk, the bow hand-tied. The whiteness set off the deep bronze tan, the brown eyes, the strong planes of his face—the taunting, sensuous lips . . . 'You made up the story— and I agreed with it—only to get me out of an awkward moment with Frank.'

'Which you pretty soon decided to accept anyway,' he said, following her through to the living room and swiftly casting his eyes about. He couldn't help but assess how she lived, if the room reflected her personality. But this time he was disappointed; save for the settee, chairs, coffee table and the expensive electronic equipment belonging to the other engineer, the room was practically bare. Her work schedule didn't give her much time to look after domestic niceties.

'If I accept a lunch date with Frank that's no business of yours,' she said, annoyed that he wasn't impressed with the room, either.

'Decided he's easier to deal with than me?' queried Max, sinking into one of the small seats and almost overpowering it. 'Frightened that if you go out with me you'll forget yourself again?'

'That's just the sort of remark I'd expect from you,' Samantha grated. 'It wouldn't occur to you, of course, that Frank and I were discussing business. It's typical of you to bring sex into everything.'

'Me?' Somehow he adopted the expression of a saint. 'My dear Samantha, we have a date. All right, an engagement for dinner,' he added, holding up a silencing hand as she was about to interrupt. 'And which of us is assuming that the motive is sexual? I always take my business associates to dinner. I've done so with your absent colleague,' he added, waving a hand towards the video gear. 'And naturally I wish to do the same with you. It makes for a better working relationship,' he went on, watching her carefully, breathing evenly, like some giant, infuriating, predatory cat.

She didn't believe him. 'Oh,' she managed to say, crossing the room to turn the radio down a bit, just for something to do. She felt alone, out of her depth. The news was just ending, the financial report was giving the state of the dollar against the yen, and she suddenly felt homesick for the more familiar battle of the dollar against the pound. 'You should have made yourself more clear,' she said at last.

'I made myself perfectly clear,' said Max, getting up and coming across to her. 'And I thought Miss Samantha Whittaker was perfectly capable of looking after herself in this business,' and the challenge lay seductively between the rich timbre of his voice and the cool, matter-of-fact expression on his face.

'All right,' she said offhandedly. 'If you really think there's anything more to discuss.' And when he looked pleased with himself, she added, 'Never let it be said that I put pleasure before business,' and he was still working that one out as she marched off to her room.

Fool! Who are you trying to kid? You want to go out to dinner with him—you know you do. Never mind Jessica. Never mind Farida. Just one night. Just one

chance . . . Samantha chose and discarded several
dresses, thrusting them back into the wardrobe
impatiently. This one was high-necked and formal,
that one was too frilly, this one didn't really suit her.
At last she pulled out a floating black chiffon
concoction, with a deep slashed neckline; very simple,
very elegant . . . Why not? Let him see she wasn't
afraid to look a woman for once.

She took her time, having a shower and damping
down her curls again, so that they would dry in
respectable order. Then she fixed her face, using a
saucy suggestion of glitter; everyone dressed up for
social occasions in Dubai—and for once she had no
intention of being outdone. At last she stepped into
the slinky dress and found some chunky gold
jewellery—but not too much. At last she gazed at her
reflection, satisfied with the contrast of red hair, lots
of creamy skin with just the suggestion of a tan, and
the simple black dress accentuating feminine curves. A
dab of perfume . . . her evening bag should be in this
drawer—yes, here it was. Ready. But still she
hesitated, her green eyes wide and thoughtful, then
she raced round tidying the bedroom, throwing towels
back into the bathroom, smoothing the rumpled
bedcover. It didn't mean anything, of course. She
wasn't committing herself—and she wouldn't let Max
come back here anyway . . . But—well, just in case!

There was no sign on her face of the few minutes'
hectic tidying up, as she went through to the sitting
room. It was getting on for nine o'clock, perhaps Max
had already gone. Then she sighed imperceptibly—no,
he hadn't left.

'I was as quick as I could be,' she began, and at the
sound of her voice he was instantly on his feet,
discarding a woman's magazine that had been the only
thing about for him to read. As it slipped to the floor
she saw the naked figure of a girl in a soap

advertisement, suitably censored by strategic black patches. But she couldn't think of any light remark, because Max was staring at her, his dark eyes half-hooded, his face inscrutable. But she could almost hear the wheels of his mind spinning round. As they faced each other across the small sitting room, she could almost imagine that he had come to some irretrievable decision. Which was crazy, of course . . .

'We'd better be going,' he said, with the ghost of a smile, 'before they give away our table.' Max Kramer wasn't angry—but he seemed to be a man with problems. And the problems had something to do with her.

It was going to be an evening to remember, despite their differences, Samantha knew that everything was going to work out all right—although for the first half hour or so they were both treading on very thin ice.

They dined in the Hyatt Regency's revolving restaurant, high above Dubai's bright tracery of lights, with jumbo jets flying practically past the window! But they flew past silently—double-glazing did a superb job.

The décor was red plush and mahogany, modern yet dim, discreet—hallowed. The clientèle was part of that exclusive, wealthy élite—the food an exotic hot and cold buffet flavoured with tempting aromatic spices— which were surprisingly sweet. Max explained what everything was—recommending several. 'I shouldn't really,' Samantha laughed, piling saffron rice, liberally sprinkled with dried fruit and pistacio nuts, on to her plate. But back at the table there was still an edge of tension between them.

'Are you enjoying working out here?' asked Max, as she began her Armenian lamb and salad.

'I thought we'd already been through all that,' she said. 'You know I'm not going to leave . . .'

'I don't mean your job—I mean out here in Dubai. Do you like living out here?'

Samantha shrugged. 'I haven't been out here long enough to find out. Bit of a contrast, isn't it? All this,' she indicated the restaurant, but also implied the wealth of ease and sophistication beyond the room. 'Expense account luxury living—coupled with some of the toughest working conditions in the world. But the people fascinate me—and the local customs. I wish I could find out more about them.'

'You will, I'm sure—if you stay.'

'I've already told you . . .'

'Okay,' he interrupted, holding up his hand in peace, 'don't let's argue.' Then he reached across the table and gently smoothed her hand. 'I don't particularly want you to leave the Gulf, as it happens.'

A herd of butterflies galloped about in her stomach. If butterflies didn't fly around in herds, it certainly felt like it! 'I thought this was supposed to be a business dinner,' she replied, removing her hand to pick up her glass of wine.

'You didn't really believe that, did you?' he said huskily, those huge brown eyes never leaving her face. For a fleeting second she saw herself running round, tidying the bedroom . . . 'And you must admit this beats an old truck in the middle of a sandstorm.'

Samantha sipped the wine—it didn't help! 'I thought you were a man of your word,' she managed to say. Well, there was no reason to make it easy for him.

'I am.'

'You said you wanted to discuss . . .'

He sighed. 'Okay.' Then he sat back, dabbed his lips with a dark red napkin, and slowly picked up his own glass of wine.

'You talked with Frank Douglas about the drill stem test at lunch today?'

'Yes.'

His face was shadowed, enigmatic. 'And he isn't going to change his mind about pulling a wet string?'

'It's my responsibility too,' she reminded him.

'Okay—correction. *You* aren't going to change your mind?'

'No,' she said firmly.

'Right, then. Subject discussed.' He put down the wine and leant forward. 'Now can we get on to a more interesting topic?' Little devils danced in his eyes, and made a beeline for her ample cleavage.

'Frank told me there'd been an accident, on an offshore rig—a friend of yours was killed.' If she was ever going to find out, it might as well be now. But her appetite had suddenly vanished and she only chased the food around her plate. 'He seems to think you hold him responsible.'

'Indirectly—yes.' Max backed off, picking up his wine again, disappearing into himself.

'But it was an accident,' she persisted.

He shrugged. 'If you like.'

'Frank says you still bear him a grudge.'

'It's common knowledge—people don't come back to life.'

'I think that's grossly unfair,' she began.

'So do I—but it's a fact of death, honey.'

'Don't try and be funny,' she snapped, and his lips thinned. He hadn't intended to be funny. 'I think it's bad enough that you continually blame Frank,' she battled on, 'but I won't allow you to transfer that blame to me.'

He didn't even try to persuade her that she had the wrong idea of him. 'So tell me about yourself,' he said, and she was amazed that he didn't blow his top. 'Go on, tell me your career to date. Show me that you're qualified to avoid getting yourself gassed, cremated or blown to pieces.'

'*What?*' she gasped.

'It's happened before. Didn't Frank tell you all the story? That friend of mine was a petroleum engineer.' He looked about to say more but decided against it. 'And I don't think that's an acceptable risk for anyone—do you?'

Samantha swallowed; she hadn't actually considered such dreadful things, but then who had? 'It's my job,' she said calmly. 'It's dangerous crossing the road. Didn't anyone ever tell you that?'

'But who crosses roads with their eyes closed?' he said, continuing the analogy. 'I've worked for your firm more times than I care to remember, and they're always the same. Always cutting corners—always wanting to do everything on the cheap. Financial problems, have they?' he interrogated.

'I don't think Mepco's affairs are any of your concern.'

'They are if they're prepared to send inexperienced personnel to work with me,' he said, for once deliberately trying not to sound sexist.

'In a minute I'll begin to think you're actually concerned for my skin,' she taunted, but with half a hope in her heart.

'I am,' he said, flooring her completely, and reaching across the table to take her hand. 'So tell me I'm wrong. Tell me about yourself. Tell me what a clever young lady you are.'

'Don't patronise!' Samantha wriggled her hand, but he wouldn't let go, and you couldn't make that much of a fuss in the Hyatt Regency! 'I'm no more—or less—clever than any reasonably qualified petroleum engineer.' And because he seemed genuinely interested, she went on to give an account of her first job after university, and then about her application to Mepco, followed by their pep-talks in Houston—and then on to Alaska for a few months, before being offered the permanent appointment down here.

'I'm impressed,' he said, gently smoothing the back of her hand with his thumb. 'But I still think I'm right—I'm sure this isn't the business for a lady . . .' His eyes were all over her, taking in the saucy curls, the creamy skin, the curving mouth and bright challenging eyes. 'I can think of far more interesting things for you to do.'

'Just because I have my kind of job, it doesn't make me any less of a woman,' she was surprised to hear herself say.

'Is that an invitation, Samantha?' And then he smiled as the beginnings of a blush crept to her cheeks. 'Never mind,' he soothed, 'it'll keep. Come on, let's go and choose a dessert.'

'But I'm already full,' she complained, glad of something mundane to say for a moment.

'Since when has that been an excuse?' and they both laughed, and wandered round to find the buffet table, which was in a different place from the first time, because the tables had been revolving quite a while since then.

'This must be the nicest restaurant in Dubai,' she sighed, when they had returned to their table and she could gaze out at the huge twinkling panorama.

'One of them,' Max smiled. 'I'd like to take you to all the others,' he added.

'Before I get blown to pieces?' and then she immediately cursed herself as a cloud passed over his face.

'I shall have to make sure that doesn't happen, shan't I?' he said quietly, then nodding with satisfaction as the waiter brought the champagne he had ordered to be served with desert.

'All this wine is going to my head.' Samantha was pleased of an opportunity of lightening the atmosphere,

as her spoon slid into the cold, tangy sorbet. Mmm . . .
delicious, but Max's eyes were solemn as he gazed at
her. 'We've done a lot of talking,' he began, 'but we
haven't really got anywhere.'

'What do you mean?' Her smile felt strangely
sideways, but he didn't seem to notice.

'We've been talking about work—about other
people. But we haven't been talking about us.'

'I didn't know there was anything to say,' she said,
with a bit of a flutter.

'Didn't you?' He went to top up her champagne
glass, but she waved him away. He refilled his own
instead, his hand perfectly steady although he had
consumed several glasses of wine with the main
course. He must be very used to entertaining on this
scale, and for a moment she tried not to imagine all
the other women he had brought up here. 'Yesterday
you seemed to have a name for it,' he went on,
returning the bottle to the ice bucket. 'A chemical
reaction, I believe you said, and I wasn't supposed
to lose any sleep over it?'

'Did you?' she asked quietly.

His eyes were perfectly serious as he answered,
'Yes.'

There was a thick silence between them; Samantha
fiddled with the stem of her wine glass and watched
another plane going in to land. 'I didn't sleep too well
either,' she admitted in the end, and Max gave her a
devastating smile that did amazing things to her nerve
ends. 'Even though I *should* hate you,' she added,
with a semi-serious grin.

'Male chauvinist that I am,' he quipped.

'Male chauvinist that you undoubtedly are,' she
agreed, taking the hand he openly offered this time,
and wondering if the whole world had gone crazy, or
only herself.

'We're two of a kind,' he said, squeezing her fingers.

'Put us together and the sparks can't help but fly. You know what you do to me, don't you?'

She nodded. Yesterday in the truck, in the sandstorm, Max Kramer's need for her had been shatteringly obvious. But was it no more than a healthy man's need for an attractive woman? For a moment she felt confused, pulled two ways—her intellect telling her to stay out of an affair that could only bring heartache, her femininity almost glad that he disapproved of the danger she could be in. For once she wanted to be possessed by such a masculine, dominant man. It didn't make sense. It was a paradox—the tension of two opposites battling in the minds of more women than herself. And what was the answer? Take one day at a time? Enjoy yourself when the opportunity arose? But was it possible to fall in love, *really* in love, and not be shattered when it came to an end? Was it possible to carry on working competently in those circumstances? But wouldn't it be equally wrong to succumb to the other alternative, which was to shut away half of herself—as she had tried to do once before?

'Why so serious?' queried Max, giving her back her hand, and asking if she had any room for some of the fresh fruit salad.

She shook her head, laughing at his appetite, trying to laugh at her own dilemma, which, even if shared with half the female population, didn't make the problem go away.

They chatted casually for the rest of the meal; she found herself telling him about growing up in London, and he explained how he had built up Gulf Services to the point where he could delegate so much now that if he wasn't careful his men would keep him entirely out of the field.

'Except when it comes to jobs like our drill stem testing,' she joked, realising that nothing on earth would keep Max Kramer behind a desk for very long.

'You're not the only one,' he taunted. 'I'm going up to Bahrain tomorrow—there's a bit of a problem on an offshore rig.'

'Be careful,' said Samantha, before suddenly realising that she didn't have the right to be concerned for his welfare.

'I'm always careful—but risks are part of my job,' and then the smile faded as they stared at each other in mutual understanding for once. 'Come on,' he said softly, after glancing round for a waiter. 'It's getting late. I think it's time we went—home?'

CHAPTER EIGHT

MAX drove Samantha home and she spent most of the journey contemplating the trap into which she was about to fall. Should she invite him in for coffee, which was asking for trouble, or should she say goodnight here in the car and be thought old-fashioned and a prude? Or maybe she should do simply what she wanted to do? And for the rest of the short ride she nestled into her seat, beat out the rhythm from the radio, and smiled a secret little smile to herself. Men like Max Kramer didn't come along very often.

In the event he forestalled her, climbing out of the car as soon as he pulled up, and coming round to open the passenger door. With accomplished ease, and without the least hint of being manipulated, Samantha found herself escorted up the little front path and automatically handed over her key for him to unlock the door. For a moment she was almost amazed that she could stand back, remove herself emotionally, and simply observe the way this lethally attractive man operated. But when she said, 'Coffee?' with as much nonchalant ease, she was entering into the dangerous game in her own right.

As she went into the kitchen, switching on the light, and blinking for a moment, she heard Max go into the sitting room, and soon there came the sound of gentle, seductive music ... In a rising panic, she filled the coffee machine and rummaged round in a drawer for the filters.

'I was just thinking,' she said, eventually carrying the tray into the sitting room and setting it down in the space he had cleared on the coffee table. 'If we were at home now, lateish in October, we'd have log fires—velvet curtains . . .'

'Icy patches on roads and early morning fog,' he finished for her, and they both laughed. Then he added seriously, 'Homesick?'

'Of course not. It's too exciting here!' Now that she had seated herself on the settee, he came across to join her. He had undone his bow tie and opened the top two buttons of his shirt, and the rearrangement gave a slow, easy casualness to his urbane sophistication. Excitement of a far different kind danced along Samantha's nerves.

'I've enjoyed tonight,' he said, accepting the coffee, sitting back—taking his time, all the while assessing her reaction.

'So have I.'

'I know.' He put his cup back on the tray, and then hers . . . 'We've been fighting far too long, wouldn't you say?' He possessed himself of her hand, playing with her fingers, smoothing her wrist. Could he feel her pulse leaping about? 'At the camel market there was this stunning redhead with the most incredible legs . . .' he grinned.

'Which you so thoroughly disapproved of,' she laughed back.

He shook his head. 'On the contrary. I like everything about you, Samantha.'

He drew her slowly closer and she found it a bit difficult breathing. 'Even though we disagree so much?' she managed to whisper.

'Forget all that.' His face was very close now, she found herself concentrating on that firm mouth—the glint of white teeth. 'This is far more important,' he concluded softly, and at last he was kissing her, slowly, tauntingly, pulling back when she wriggled with delight, gazing down into her deep green eyes.

'Truce?' he said with a smile, that did amazing things to his face.

'Temporary or permanent?' she asked with a wicked grin, but he didn't seem to want to pick up the joke.

His eyes were serious as he said, 'Permanent, I think, don't you?' and there was a special secretness in his voice, a sharing—a coming together.

Samantha reached for him, coiling her hand around his neck, drawing him closer, knowing that she loved him beyond measure, that it was right for them to be together . . . 'Love me,' she heard herself whisper, and his response was a husky groan as he bent to kiss her again.

The kiss went on and on, deeper, darker. How good he felt beneath her searching palms as they slid under his jacket and up the strong column of his back. But she couldn't get close enough, they had too many clothes on . . .

'You're quite a lady,' he whispered, breaking the kiss at last, but only because he wanted to nuzzle her ear, then nibble his way down her neck.

With a shiver and a little cry of delight, she flung her head back against the settee, savouring the exquisite torture of his searching hands and lips. He was sliding the dress off her shoulders now, his greedy brown eyes feasting on the lengthening cleavage that was peeping into view. Then he began smoothing the skin with the back of his hand, nudging the dress lower, searching for her back zip . . . sliding it slowly downwards.

'That's better,' he murmured, dangerous lights burning in his eyes as he noted her approval. The dress was slipping even lower . . .

'Max, I . . .' she began, but her voice faded out.

'Yes, darling . . .?' But he didn't wait for her to continue, before helping the gossamer black chiffon finally to fall to her waist. 'Beautiful,' he breathed, and all she could do was stare at the tense muscle jerking in his cheek.

'Max,' she tried again. 'I haven't done this kind of thing before,' she wanted to add, but again the words wouldn't come out. They sounded childish, naïve. Not the sort of thing a woman of her experience would want to admit.

'I know—I want you too, but we'll wait a little longer, yes? Make the moment last . . .' And now he bent to kiss the tip of her breasts, slowly, sensuously, that had her moaning with delight, burrowing her fingers into his shoulders until he began tugging with gentle teeth. And that was just too much, she couldn't stand any more. White hot needles of desire flooded through her with every heartbeat. How did he know exactly what to do?

Fool! Reality laughed at her. Max Kramer knew exactly what to do because he had done it countless times before with exciting, extrovert women like Jessica, and with sophisticated, experienced women like Farida. And how many more besides? And suddenly Samantha knew that she didn't want to be one of the links in his line of conquests. She wanted to be more than that—special. Because something had happened to her yesterday in the sandstorm; it was as if the hot, violent wind had blown away all her fears about men, about her ability to cope sexually with a man on equal footing. Yesterday, the screaming sand had stripped bare her emotions and allowed her to see herself as she wanted to be; a warm, loving, exciting woman—prepared to abandon her independence for the right man. For a while out there in the desert, she had felt strong enough to fit the two most important things in her life into one existence—one reality. She could cope with her career—*and* with loving a man like Max. The two weren't mutually exclusive . . .

But that had been yesterday, out in the wild,

untamed wilderness, when the world had seemed to be
full of just the two of them. But today, she was aware
of her own vulnerability. To have an affair with Max,
because she knew he wouldn't consider any other kind
of relationship, would be a declaration of her love . . .

She moaned softly as he began nuzzling her ear
now, his warm hand coaxing, caressing.

. . . But it would also be necessary for him to love
her. He would have to love her so that he would care
enough to learn to understand her. Really to get to
know her as a person. Instinctively Samantha knew
that she would want to be *friends* with her lover.
Partners. Which seemed a very strange thought . . .

'What's the matter?' he whispered, his voice still
deep and sensuous, still sounding pleased with
himself.

'I was just thinking.' She eased him away and
began pulling up her dress. He didn't seem to mind.
Did he think she was about to suggest they went to
bed?

'Thinking what?' His fingers were in her hair,
flicking the wayward curls into place, humouring
her . . .

'That we ought to be friends.'

He looked mildly thunderstruck. 'I think we've
left it a bit late for that.' His eyes were all over her.
'Samantha, I want you.'

But how many other women did he want as well?
not that he didn't admit as much. He openly escorted
both Jessica and Farida. Obviously the women in his
life had to be prepared to accept each other. And
Samantha knew that for her it would be impossible. If
she let him stay the night she would have a couple of
hours of shattering lovemaking, of that there was little
doubt! But what then? A brief kiss goodbye? Hearing
his car drive away? Or would she wake up in the
morning and find him gone? His work could take him

at a moment's notice anywhere in the Gulf—anywhere in the world. And when he came back he would have other women on his list to see before he got round to Samantha. And she couldn't live with the doubt—the misery. She *couldn't*.

'I—think you'd better go,' she said at last, somehow finding the strength to move him away.

'Oh, come on!' His tone suggested that he knew she was teasing him. He thought she was enjoying the game. He thought she was as experienced as himself. 'Darling . . .' he tried again, but she moved along the settee.

'It's late.'

He shrugged the argument aside, glancing at his watch, but instead of proving her wrong, he looked genuinely surprised to discover it was almost two o'clock.

'It is late—you're right,' he said. 'Perhaps I ought to go. I don't like leaving Sue-Lee alone in the house all night.' And that wasn't the answer she wanted to hear from him either. Why didn't he protest? Didn't he *mind* leaving? 'Besides,' he went on, moving up beside her, resting a gentle hand on her shoulder, 'I think we deserve something better than a quick tumble, don't you?' He briefly kissed her warming cheek. 'Silly to behave like a couple of kids. We'll have a weekend away somewhere. Have you been over to Khor Fakkan?'

'Er—no, not yet.' The conversation wasn't going exactly as she had imagined. She hadn't intended him to believe that her former experience in these matters had told her it would be more fun to wait.

'You'll love it,' he coaxed, looking as if he was liking the idea himself. 'Good beaches. Several good hotels. And forty-eight beautiful hours to do exactly what we like . . .'

'I don't get weekends off,' she said hurriedly.

'Then we'll wait until your twenty-eight days are up—have even longer over there . . .'

'I—I'll let you know.' Fool, why didn't you say 'No'?

'I'll phone when I get back,' he said with a smile.

'Back from where?' Samantha couldn't help herself.

'I told you—Bahrain. I fly out tomorrow. No, today,' he corrected. 'In four and a half hours, to be precise.' And then with a disconcerting smile he kissed her again and said, 'You're quite right, darling—four hours isn't half enough time. Don't come to the door, I'll see myself out.' And he did, while she was still sitting on the settee and staring into space.

Max Kramer had gone this time—but how long before he came back? Came back to carry on where he left off. And now that he had gone, didn't it feel the most important thing in the world that he should have stayed?

The phone rang just as Samantha poured the omelette into the pan. Damn! She turned off the gas and ran into the sitting room. Max had been gone five days—but no, it wouldn't be him calling, not now, would it?

It was Mepco's operator with a call for her, and she instantly recognised John Trent's voice as he spoke her name.

'You're working late. I was just about to have supper,' she added with a grimace.

'Sorry—won't keep you long.' John sounded excited. 'I stayed on to run through this afternoon's samples . . .'

'And?' she prompted, already knowing what was coming.

'We're there. Ready for the test. You can give Kramer the go-ahead as soon as you like.'

Samantha was doing some rapid calculations. It would take at least thirty-six hours to remove the pipe so that the drill stem-testing equipment could replace the usual drilling bit. Thirty-six hours brought them up to Thursday morning, maybe the afternoon before the well would be clear . . . 'Max Kramer's still in Bahrain at the moment, or so I believe,' she added hastily. 'But I'll contact him somehow. Make sure he's back and ready to leave by—shall we say—very early Thursday morning?'

'Fine. See you tomorrow,' said John.

Samantha put down the phone and picked it up again. She was beginning to feel sick—her heart was banging about as she dialled Max's office number, just in case he was there. For three days she had been dreading this moment. It was three days since she had spoken to Farida. Three days in which she had been trying to forget Max Kramer.

His phone was switched on to automatic answer, an emergency number was given. Samantha scribbled it down. It was probably his home number. But she dialled it, imagining it ringing in that sumptuous living room that she had visited just after they had first met—the time she was stuck in the sand and the garage people had never turned up. So much seemed to have happened since then. She wasn't even the same person . . . Now perhaps the bungalow was empty—the room in darkness . . .

'Hullo!' The ringing had stopped abruptly, and a woman's voice came clearly down the line. Samantha recognised it immediately, and she had to close her eyes for a moment and take a deep breath.

She gave her name. 'Is Max there?'

'Er—Samantha, it is me, Farida. You are well, yes?'

'Yes,' she squeaked, appalled at the idea of a social chat. 'I'm sorry to bother you so late.'

'It is no bother.' The Syrian's lovely smile seemed to travel down the line. 'But I am afraid Max has not yet arrived back from Bahrain,' she explained in her precise little voice. 'His plane lands at midnight.'

And look who'll be waiting at home for him, Samantha thought wretchedly. But she had known that since Sunday—she couldn't have expected anything less.

'It doesn't matter,' she managed to say, and briefly left a message giving the relevant details, and saying she would phone him at his office the following morning.

Then she put the phone down, plodded back into the kitchen, scraped the cold, congealed mess of an omelette into the bin, then sat down at the table and had a good cry.

The first couple of days after Max had left had been bad enough. One moment wishing she hadn't sent him away, the next moment glad that she had. Wondering how she would cope with him when he came back. Wondering if she would have the courage *not* to go away with him for the weekend. She had hated her weakness, her mixed up feelings for the man. But at least she had been able to think about Max as a possibility—as perhaps being part of her life for some time to come.

But all that had ended on Sunday when Samantha had met Kate again at the hospital pool and they had again been joined by Farida.

This time there had been no emergency to take the two women away, this time Farida stretched out in her white bikini, her slim body deeply tanned, her long dark hair swept up into a bun. Her sunglasses were huge—a joke—her bracelets thick, chunky, pure twenty-two-carat gold. Like Max, she was an enigma; dark, serious, quiet eyes hiding behind a friendly smile. Samantha couldn't help but like her . . .

'Peace,' Farida had said, as the late afternoon sun slanted beneath their awning, and Kate, on the far side of her, began smoothing suncream into her legs. 'No bells ringing—no patients needing me,' she continued.

'Careful!' Kate muttered, and they all laughed.

'It is true, I am getting old,' Farida went on. 'Thirty-two is very old for a woman to remain single in my country. At last I think I am truly looking forward to getting married. To leave the hospital for a while will be—pleasant.'

'Married?' stammered Samantha, before she could stop herself.

'I didn't realise you'd named the day,' said Kate, who obviously knew all about it.

'It is about time—no?' said Farida, and the two of them had laughed knowingly, but Samantha had decided it was time for another swim.

'But what about your career?' she heard Kate say, as she hurried over to the edge of the pool.

'I will take off two or three years—to have children. It is expected. But then—yes, back to work—although what my parents will say . . .'

But Samantha didn't want to hear what her parents would say. And she didn't want to hear Kate say how lucky Farida was to be marrying a man like Max. Samantha had guessed for a little while now that Kate rather fancied Max.

Of course, Max was the man Farida was about to marry, wasn't he? It was obvious. But any little doubt she had clung on to vanished as soon as she had made that phone call to his home. Farida was waiting for him. He wasn't expected until after midnight. Farida was a respectable middle-class Syrian lady. There wasn't anything more to say, except to agree with her; the sooner she married Max, the better.

Samantha dried her eyes at last, poked in the fridge for something else to eat, and tried to get herself together. By the time she met Max for the stem testing he must have no idea that inside her heart was breaking in two.

When she managed to speak to him on the phone

the following day, he seemed pleasant, but pre-
occupied. Businesslike as they discussed the plans for
the journey out to the rig—yet indicating in no way
anything that had passed between them before he went
to Bahrain. But then he wouldn't, would he? He might
even be regretting the pass he had made after their
evening at the Hyatt Regency. Farida had stood him
up the night before, she remembered, even if it was
supposed to have been because of an emergency. Had
Max taken Samantha out simply to make Farida
jealous? And had his strategy worked? Was that why
she was suddenly announcing her impending marriage?

When she put the phone down, Samantha glanced at
the office calendar and mentally crossed off the days
she had already worked of her twenty-eight-day tour.
Just over two more weeks to go, and then she could
get out of the Gulf for a month. But was that long
enough to get over a man like Max? Would he be
married when she returned?

It was still dark on Thursday morning as she packed
the car with the minimum of gear essential for the next
few days. There was a sleeping bag and a couple of
towels. Spare sandals and two fat paperbacks to read
during all the hanging about, and the roll bag with her
toilet things and clothes was already bursting at the
seams. She had rammed in three pairs of jeans, at least
half a dozen tee-shirts and all the underwear she could
grab. It was bad enough in Dubai with showers and
more changes of clothes in a day than the Queen! But
out in the desert it would seem even hotter, and she
hadn't remembered seeing as much as a hand-basin in
her room.

A grey dawn was giving way to a low, orange sun
peeping between tall buildings as she drove into town.
But it was still relatively cool and it made a change to

drive without air-conditioning and therefore with the windows wound down. As she whizzed through the deserted, early morning streets, the warm wind blew pleasantly through her curls. Maybe she was getting acclimatised. Even a fortnight ago, when she had arrived in the Gulf, she would have found it too hot to enjoy, even at this time in the morning.

She met the others in Mepco's underground car park and transferred her gear to the boot of Frank's car.

'Expecting trouble?' he quipped, at the size of her bags. 'All set for staying out there a month?'

She laughed, then her stomach flipped over as a Gulf Services truck eased its way down the ramp. Then John arrived and doors were opening, men climbing out—everyone muttering a jaundiced early morning greeting to each other—but there was no sign of Max.

'Kramer decided we can do without him?' queried Frank, with a certain satisfaction, but one of the Gulf men shook his head.

'He's taking the kid over to stay with a friend. Said he'd be here at seven.'

Frank grunted and helped John fit his bag into the boot. Samantha decided 'the kid' was Sue-Lee, and she remembered Max saying that he didn't like leaving her alone. But it was nearly seven now . . .

And then, as if on cue, the big black Chevrolet nosed its way into the underground car park, and Max climbed out, looking tall, lean and powerful in white, tightly fitting jeans and green and white loose-fitting shirt.

He gave a swift nod in the direction of the Mepco group, listened while one of his men brought him up to date with some details, then retrieved his own holdall from the back of his car and tossed it into his truck. Then he strolled over to Frank.

He moved with the slow, lethal grace of a confident,

athletically fit man. Samantha couldn't keep her eyes off him—yet he had hardly given her more than a glance. This was the man who had kissed her, who had wanted to make love to her. Her treacherous memory rewound back to the evening at her bungalow . . . The way he had slid the dress off her shoulders . . . down to her waist. She could almost feel his lips on her breasts . . .

'We're still planning to pull a wet string?' he asked Frank, in the manner of a man giving someone a last chance.

'Yep,' said the American.

Max's eyes remained hard. 'Okay, let's go.' And to Samantha's utmost relief, he turned away and climbed into the driving seat of the Gulf Services truck. For a dreadful moment she had thought he might have been travelling with them. And she could imagine what it would be like to be cooped up in the same car, maybe both in the back seat—touching, having to speak to each other . . .

'Going off the idea?' John was saying, and after a moment Samantha realised he was speaking to her. 'Would Madam care to join us?' he tried again, and she realised with a rush of embarrassment that everyone else was in their vehicles and raring to go. She had just been standing there like a dummy . . .

'Now you'll find out why we only make you work for twenty-eight days on the trot,' said Frank, in a mocking voice of doom. But as the little convoy pulled out into the sunlight, Samantha sank back in her seat and closed her eyes. Luckily Frank would never guess just how rough this trip was going to be for her.

The car reached the rig first, which gave Samantha time to dump her things in her office-cum-bedroom and stroll across to the opposite Portakabin which was Frank's office. But before she had time to pour herself a coffee, the truck rolled up and the place seemed to be overrun with Gulf Services men who looked as if they wanted to chat her up, but for once not sure where to begin. They obviously weren't used to seeing a woman out in the desert, either.

Next the tool pusher came to tell them that the bit was already out of the hole, So Max didn't let anyone rest for long, but wanted to get up on the drilling floor and get things moving.

'I'm coming too,' said Samantha, making for the door. 'I'll just get my hat,' and for a second Max actually looked at her over the bobbing heads with a thoughtful expression, and then he had finally given her a nod.

So she scurried across the dusty track that separated the two rows of cabins, and leapt the three wooden steps up to her door. For a moment she stood in the centre of the little room, revelling in its coolness, relieved that there was air-conditioning out here, her eyes going round the cramped quarters which were just big enough for a desk, chair, cupboard and couple of bunks. For once it paid off being a woman; if she had been a man she would have had to double up. There was still the washing facilities to find, and opening the cupboard at last, she brought down her hard hat from the high shelf. She laughed at the forgotten decorations the men had stuck on to it, with Hot Lips especially emblazoned at the front. Then she kicked off her sandals, changed them for trainers, and rummaged in the cupboard again for her tough pair of protective gloves. She knew from experience that the metal ladder up to the drilling floor could get pretty hot.

Max was already supervising his men as their equipment was being installed on the drill floor. Samantha had climbed up slowly, passing the first floor with its huge blow-out preventers, which she hoped would never have to be used when she was about! And then upwards, stepping lightly on to the drill floor, but having to take her hat off for a second to wipe her forehead with the back of her hand. Goodness, it was hot! And if it was hot here, what must it be like for the derrick man, high up on his platform, swinging the long sections of pipe into place? No wonder drilling crews were some of the toughest men going. For a job like this they would need to be.

She stayed quietly out of the way while Max and his assistant fitted the special equipment that would take the reservoir sample. The two men worked well together, but instead of the engineering techniques, Samantha found herself staring at the dark line of perspiration gradually staining the back of Max's shirt. Taut muscles strained against taut material, the long length of his thighs was accentuated as he braced himself to wield the giant tongs . . . At last she dragged her eyes away, she mustn't keep thinking about him— she *mustn't*, so she wandered over and chatted to one of the roustabouts for a moment, laughing at his cheeky comments, aware that with her about they were all working under severe strain of keeping their language clean.

But then Max was shouting some orders to one of the lads, and at last all the equipment was assembled and ready to go into the well. She knew it would take thirty-six hours for the test tool to reach the bottom— and another thirty-six hours to come up again after he had carried out his test. But already Samantha had learned that in this job you contrasted important, knife-edged decisions and a certain amount of danger with the boring necessity of having to hang around for hours in pretty tough conditions.

She didn't see much of Max the first day, not alone, anyway. Not with any chance to talk to each other. Would he offer some sort of explanation? He must know she had spoken to Farida . . . Or was he keeping out of her way on purpose—was he embarrassed by the situation?

The drill pipe started going down in the late afternoon. A truck went back to Dubai and she could have had a lift home, coming back in the morning. But Max didn't go back—and she had no intention of looking as if she wanted a soft option. And Frank wasn't shifting while Max Kramer was operating on a Mepco well . . . In the end Samantha shut herself in her office and tried to get on with some work.

And so it dragged on until the thirty-six hours were up and she was halfway through her pile of clean tee-shirts and undies.

'They're ready for the test,' someone had banged on her door, when it was hardly light on Saturday morning. But even then there was nothing to do, except stand around while the Gulf Services group got on with the job. Fascinating to think that from the surface, Max could manipulate his testing equipment—practically *feel* his way delicately through each operation.

'Bet you twenty dirhams he gets the sample out with no contamination,' said John, leaning against the side of a Portakabin and ruefully rubbing his early morning stubbly chin.

'Done,' was all Samantha said, as someone brought them huge mugs of coffee, because in a minute, when the operation was over, her worries would begin. Right now Max was up there in charge, doing things his way—and it was his responsibility. But soon he would come down—come here into Frank's office and say it was time to start pulling the string.

She was right. He came back into the office before giving the final order. 'You want them to go ahead without mud?'

'You know perfectly well that there isn't any made

up,' she said wearily. Why did he have to go on about it?

'I'm prepared to wait,' he said.

'Well, we're not. Please go ahead,' she said, glad that for once Frank wasn't here and she could tell him straight herself . . .

Saturday was hell. Now they had reached the danger point. Now there would be gas sucked up with the reservoir sample . . . And if it expanded on the way up . . . If the well gave a hiccup—with no mud down there to hold things back. If a blow-out preventer valve should malfunction . . . Samantha seemed to spend all day watching the men slowly removing long lengths of pipe, aware that every time they took off the wet plug there was nothing between the reservoir sample and fresh air. These thirty-six hours were going to be tough to live through—and not only for herself, it seemed. Because all day Saturday and well into the night, Max prowled around, up on the rig with the changing crews, making sure everything was done as he wanted, that no short cuts were taken. Thirty-six hours while once again the drill pipe was laboriously extracted . . . Thirty-six hours for Samantha to pray that she had made the right decision.

They let her sleep late on Sunday, but she just made breakfast, and then strolled back to her office, stopping as usual to stare up at the towering rig, shielding her eyes as another length of pipe was unshackled and stashed in its rack by the derrick man. She felt hot and dusty already, her tee-shirt was sticking to her. She needed a shower and another change of clothes . . .

Her office was icy cool and dim as she stepped out of the heat and sank into the chair, tension making her feel tired, the continual grinding of the machines getting to her for a moment. And yet in a way she welcomed the tiredness because it made it more difficult to think about . . .

There was a knock at her door; how soon privacy was shattered out here. She called out, 'Come in,' expecting Frank or John. Either way she certainly didn't expect Max Kramer to step slowly into the room.

He looked tired, the strain of the last couple of days seemed to be telling on him. He was wearing beige jeans now, and a loose, bush-style shirt which was half open, displaying a strong neck, auburn chest hairs . . . his skin glistened with the heat. He looked as if he had missed out on shaving that morning; a dark chin and sweat-soaked hair gave him the rough, Neolithic image that she had only guessed at before. Here was the man behind the urbane sophistication of downtown Dubai. This was the Max Kramer whose name was called when there was trouble.

'What do you want?' she asked, in a rather tight little voice, not really sure how she could speak to him without breaking down. If he began to argue with her—or worse, if he pretended that nothing had happened between them the other night . . .

'I've been wondering why you've been avoiding me,' he said at last, closing the door behind him. 'I thought we had a few plans to make.' He smiled briefly, but it soon vanished. 'Or have you changed your mind about coming away to Khor Fakkan?'

CHAPTER NINE

SAMANTHA stared at Max. He was out of his mind! Did he really imagine she would go away with him for a weekend when he was practically about to be married?

'I haven't been avoiding you,' she said, shuffling papers on her desk. 'I just don't think we have anything to say to each other—do you?'

'Obviously—or I wouldn't be here.' He came and perched on the edge of her desk, stretching out long legs, crossing his ankles, staring down at her with those huge brown eyes that were shadowed now—shrewd.

She had no intention of playing cat and mouse, she would throw back his challenge right away. 'I saw Farida at the swimming pool the other afternoon,' she began, somehow finding the courage to stare him right in the eye. She hoped he couldn't hear her heart banging about. 'She told me she was making plans for the wedding.'

'Pressure from home,' he explained lightly, as if it was of no more interest than the weather forecast. Samantha looked around wildly for something to throw at him. 'She comes from an eminent Syrian family,' he went on calmly, 'who seem proud of her success—but old habits die hard. Now they've persuaded her it's time to settle down and have a family.'

'How nice,' she snapped, rage stifling a sob. Max Kramer could actually sit there discussing his future wife while trying to make Samantha his next mistress!

Max shrugged. 'It's their way,' he said ambiguously, and Samantha frowned. 'They had the husband lined up since they were both this high.' He spread a hand to indicate the height of a very young child. 'I hope she'll be happy, she's certainly going into it with her eyes open.'

Samantha continued staring at him for a moment longer; it felt as if someone had just kicked her in the stomach. Her brain was suddenly reduced to the state of cotton-wool, but through it all spun the crazy notion that she had been wrong—that Max wasn't Farida's prospective husband. He wasn't going to marry her . . .

'But I don't see what Farida has to do . . .' he began, then those shrewd eyes picked up her discomfiture, and a disbelieving smile broke out on his face. 'You didn't think,' he began, 'not Farida and me? . . .'

'No—of course not,' she tried to cover her confusion, but he didn't believe her.

'No wonder I got the frosty reception,' he said, reaching down for her hand and slowly drawing her to her feet. 'You were upset?'

She didn't answer.

'Good,' he grinned, and with a swift glance out of the window to make sure no one could see them, he eased her firmly against him and lowered his lips to her own. Firm hands slid down her back and smoothed her bottom, and all the anger and sorrow melted out of her; she was dissolving, disappearing into him . . .

Her hands went around his neck, burrowing into his damp hair. Her whole body was intoxicated by the feel of him, the musky, virile smell of him. He tasted of sand and sun—and a dangerous potent strength. As she wriggled into him he groaned softly and broke the kiss.

'I've missed you,' he whispered, nibbling her ear. 'It's been a long week.'

The longest week I've ever known, she silently

agreed. Still, round and round spun the amazing
knowledge that he wasn't going to marry Farida—and
even crazier, didn't seem to be shattered that she was
out to marry someone else. Somehow that didn't feel
right, but Samantha had no time to consider it further,
because he was speaking again.

'I've been thinking,' he was saying softly, those
taunting hands moving over her possessively, making
her knees weak—making her shiver . . . He grinned in
satisfaction . . . 'I've been thinking—that if a week
without you was hell, what is every other month going
to be like?'

'What do you mean?' she asked, then gasped and
playfully hit him. 'Stop it—someone might come in!'
She tried to pull out of his arms, but he wouldn't let
her go.

'You're working a twenty-eight-day back-to-back.'
Dark eyes gleamed as they lingered with pleasure
on her vee-necked tee-shirt that clung in all the right
places. 'Twenty-eight days here—and twenty-eight
days back in the U.K. I don't think I'm going to like
that,' he said, snaking their hips together until her
eyes widened in growing excitement. 'I think it would
be much nicer if you spent all your twenty-eight days'
leave with me.'

'With you?' she repeated breathlessly.

'We'll still have our weekend away first,' he assured
her swiftly. 'Do it properly. Spoil ourselves. Agreed?' he
added, head on one side, prompting her acquiescence.

'Agreed,' she mumbled, perfectly aware of what she
was implying—but then there didn't seem anything
else to say. The thought of spending a weekend away
with Max Kramer was too unbelievable to be missed.

'And afterwards,' he went on, 'I think we deserve to
give ourselves a little more time to get to know each
other—and you can only get to know someone if you
live with them.'

'Aren't you rushing things a bit?' she said, breaking out of his arms, and this time he let her go.

'Am I?' His face was suddenly grave.

She shrugged. No, maybe it wasn't for him if he had spent all week thinking about it. But for her it was a bit of a bombshell—only ten minutes ago she had seriously thought he was engaged to someone else.

And then she made herself think of what he was really offering. Not love. Not marriage. Simply to share his home—share his bed. But then there would be nothing simple about that!

'I—don't know what to say. We'd hardly see each other. You away sometimes for weeks on end, me out on the rig—working all hours.' She turned away and stared out of the window at the other row of dusty Portakabins.

'But only for twenty-eight days at a time,' he reminded her, coming across the tiny room and turning her round in his arms. 'Think of those other twenty-eight days, when you could stay at home and wait for me . . .'

'We'd argue—you know we would,' she said frantically, because there seemed only one thing better than sleeping with Max for the weekend—and that was sleeping with him for ever. But he didn't mean that. He wasn't offering her a permanent relationship.

'Yet think how nice it will be when we make up,' he continued, smoothing her bare arm, his fingers taunting the sensitive spot inside her elbow. 'And we don't have any differences where it counts most. You want me, Sam—and you know damn well I want you. We do something to each other. You're not a kid. You've been around a bit. You know how it is when a couple really make it good together.' She opened her mouth to say she didn't know anything of the sort, but nothing came out. 'Something like that doesn't happen every day,' he went on when it was clear she wanted to remain silent. 'It's special. And we've both known from the beginning. That day at the camel market, I couldn't keep my eyes off you. And if you still needed convincing, then you sure found out that afternoon in the truck.'

'In the sandstorm?' she muttered.

'Where else?' His eyes were all over her, willing her to agree, transmitting the sexual tension that she could see beating out of him. Suddenly the room wasn't big enough for the two of them. She jumped up, breathing quickly, wiping her damp forehead with the back of her hand. It was very hot in here. Had the air-conditioning broken down?

'It's all right, honey, I'm not trying to hustle you.' Max stepped away from her, pulling out her chair—inviting her to sit down again. 'We'll take one step at a time, yes? We'll have our weekend first, and then we'll see how quickly you make up your mind. Are we agreed on Khor Fakkan?' he went on, when she didn't reply, 'This weekend coming? Or the next? When do you finish this tour?'

'Er—next weekend—no, the weekend after . . . I—I'm not sure.'

He smiled indulgently. 'Perhaps you'd like to check your diary,' and with horror she realised that he imagined her doubts about choosing a date were of a purely biological nature.

'I—didn't mean that,' she said, flushing to the roots of her hair, and before she turned away she saw him giving her a curious little look. Lord, what was she getting into? Max Kramer's experience in these matters was only too evident. And he thought she was as used to discussing these things with her current man—as he obviously was with his current woman.

The noise from outside suddenly closed in on her. The great winding gear bringing up the pipe, section after section, the ceaseless grind of progress—yet taking place in here, in this little cabin, was the age-old struggle of the sexes that had been going on since time began . . . And she did want Max desperately—she did.

'I think we both ought to go away as soon as possible,' Max was saying now. 'Give ourselves a little treat when we've finished this lot. Celebrate?' And it was the smile that did it, a smile that broke down all the barriers she was building up in her mind. Maybe they were on opposing sides out here on the rig—maybe he did disapprove of her career. But the smile lighting up his face and warming his eyes told her that nothing could come between them—that they were meant for each other.

'Why not?' she said wickedly. 'The very first weekend I can scrape together . . .' and he was just about to scoop her into his arms when there was a strange noise outside, sort of like a wild, screaming jet engine getting closer and closer . . . followed by the sudden silence of the engines immediately cutting out.

'What the . . .' Max frowned as they stared at each other. Then a split second later he knew exactly what had happened. '*God!*' he roared, rage filling his face that had suddenly turned white. In two steps he was wrenching open the door and Samantha was right behind him, tumbling out into the heat and brilliant light. And she almost died on the spot. *Oh no!* The very worst thing possible had happened. Max had been right. The well, her *first* well, had blown!

'Stay here!' Max shouted, running across to the rig, as Frank came out of his office, hollering like mad, waving his arms at someone, running after Max. But what could they do—what could they *do*!

Samantha sank down on her steps and stared hopelessly. Straight through the middle of the rig, and high up into the air, rose a thin column of thick black oil, which had been caught by the wind and blown away from the camp, thank goodness. But had anyone been hurt? How had it happened? Why hadn't the wet plugs worked? The well was blowing out through the drill pipe!

And it was all her fault—her fault. Max had warned her that without mud the well could kick. And she had been so sure—so confident. It was a chance in a thousand, these days . . . And through her turmoil came the steady roar of escaping gas and oil. Even with every engine shut down there was still the grave risk of fire! She was instantly on her feet; Max had gone up there!

'We call in the experts.' Frank's fist came crashing down on the table, around which sat all the experienced heads of each section. The rig superintendent, the safety officer, among others. With everything shut down the air-conditioning wasn't running and the heat in the metal Portakabin was close on unbearable. They had been in here for over an hour now, assessing the situation, and it did seem the safest idea to bring in the experts. It was their job to deal with a blow-out. They had the experience.

'But how much will it cost?' she asked, imagining what Houston would have to say about that.

'More than we can afford,' Frank grated, 'but there's no way we can contain that flow——'

'I can,' said Max, and he glared at Frank, fully prepared for an all-out war.

'Is that so?' said the American, wiping the back of his neck with a handkerchief and breaking open a can of Coke. 'And would you mind telling me why I should even consider you when there's a crew in Houston . . .'

'Okay, call in the big boys,' said Max aggressively. 'But let me remind you of one or two things first.

One—no one's been hurt up till now, but the longer we leave it the greater the risk of fire. *Two*,' he emphasised, as Frank seemed about to interrupt, 'there may be a plane filled with emergency equipment on the runway at Houston, but they still have to get Customs clearance. It's going to take at least two days for them to get here. And you know as well as I do,' his eyes flashed dangerously, 'that the first day they're here they'll just stand around looking at the well. And it's *your* time—*your* money. Ask yourself if Mepco might be interested in me doing a quick job.'

Frank glared back, and Samantha's stomach tied itself into a tight knot. 'So tell me what you have in mind,' said Frank, and Max settled back in his chair again.

'Get a new control valve from stores. Swing it over the well, while it's still open, of course, screw it into the drill pipe—then wind it shut.'

'You're nuts!' Frank roared, and Max's lips thinned.

'Those things weigh a ton,' Samantha tried to placate in a soothing voice. 'How would you get it up there?'

'Block and tackle.'

'But you haven't got any lifting power, man,' Frank barged on. 'The engines are switched off, remember. You can't expect the crews to go up there and help—that sort of work isn't in their contract.'

'I'm well aware of that,' Max snapped. 'And I have no intention of asking any of my men to work up there either. But there's nothing to stop them hauling on a chain if it's long enough and they can stay twenty or thirty yards back.'

The rig superintendent nodded, Frank fiddled with a pen, everyone else sat with strained faces. Samantha's mind was spinning—could it work? . . . and as the tension built up again, it was Max's turn to crash his fist down on the table.

'At least let me try,' he shouted. 'Give me half a day. I don't want a fire out there. I don't want *anybody* killed!' And his burning eyes glared straight at Samantha, the dreadful anger in his face telling her without doubt that he held her completely responsible for the whole affair. And she was suddenly frightened for him. Why couldn't someone else try to cap it? But there wasn't anyone else, was there?

'I'll give you to six o'clock,' said Frank gruffly, and without a glance or word to anyone, Max charged out of the room and Frank reached for the radio telephone.

Samantha mumbled some excuse to John and ran back to her own room, flinging herself on the bunk and staring up at the ceiling. In her mind she went over and over what Max would have to do, with everyone else standing clear. And supposing there was a spark? Supposing something scraped on the metal, then the whole thing would go up like a torch . . . But she wouldn't cry. It was too horrifying for that. Why couldn't Frank do it? After all, he was Company man. But even she could see there wouldn't be much sense in that. He wasn't fit enough to do a thing like that on his own. But couldn't he at least help Max? But then she realised that Max wouldn't have confidence to work with him. She blew a cooling breath over her face and plucked at her damp tee-shirt. Why did she have to be so useless?

For an hour she sat and tried to think of something, drinking a lukewarm can of orange squash, wreathed in guilt . . . And slowly, slowly it dawned on her that Max couldn't cope on his own—the pressure of that oil made it impossible.

She was just about to rush out and tell him, but collided with someone equally in a hurry to see her. It was Max. For a second she hadn't recognised him in his green rubberised protective suit.

'I've just realised,' she began, not protesting as he practically picked her up and deposited her back in the office. 'You can't do it on your own. When you swing that valve over the oil, it'll take at least two. And we can't ask any of the contract men to take that kind of risk—we don't have the right.'

'I know,' he said, and his voice was icy calm. He had closed the door behind him, and in the stifling room she could almost taste the physical magnetism of the man. 'That's why I've come to see you.' His eyes were hard, his face grim. 'You're the engineer round here. The buck has nowhere else to go. They'll soon be ready to haul the valve up,' and with only the slightest hesitation, he added, 'Get your slickers on!'

He was gone, and she didn't have time to feel sick. But her stupid hands were shaking as she struggled into the unwieldy suit, relieved that they had found one nearer her size. But it was still too big, the jacket slid off her shoulders as she dealt with flaps and zips. Finally she grabbed her hard hat, rammed it on, then pulled the rubber hood up over the top. She remembered the boots, and the thick gloves, still putting them on as she ran outside, lurched down the steps, and staggered over to the small crowd of men.

Max took her arm. 'Let's get going.' And there was no warmth in his voice, just a strong determination that they were going to succeed.

Samantha felt weighed down, it was very difficult moving, but somehow she clambered up the metal ladder, trying not to think about sparks, forcing herself to stay calm and do whatever Max said. She had gone in front of him, so she reached the drill floor first, and there it was, the evil jet of oil spurting upwards, no bigger round than a large dinner plate, but with a force behind it, that as she stepped nearer, gave her the feeling that it wanted to suck her up with it—like a giant, prehistoric Hoover.

She backed off as Max clambered up and gave the signal for the men on the ground to start hauling their chain.

'We'll get the valve up as far as here, then I'll explain what I want you to do,' he shouted, and she nodded as the tackle squeaked and groaned and the giant valve was brought all the way up by manpower. The angle of the chain was such that as soon as the valve cleared the level of the drilling floor, they could fairly easily swing it over towards them, although it bumped and scraped a bit because it wasn't equally balanced. Telling her to stand back, Max gave another signal and the chain went slack and the valve banged down on the floor. He immediately unshackled it, then climbed up to the block and tackle and moved its position, so that it was much nearer the jet of disgusting oil that smelt of bad eggs.

He was climbing down now, rearranging the shackles, raising his arm for the signal to lift again, then giving the 'hold it there' sign when the valve had reached a couple of feet from the floor. It was an enormous thing, its opening much, much bigger than the oil flow it had to cap. Samantha realised they only had to cut their way through the jet once. Then the oil would be able to flow quite freely through the valve while Max fastened it down. How was he going to do that? But she didn't have time to work it out, because he was speaking to her again.

'We'll swing it,' he said. 'Once. Twice. Then the third time we'll go through the jet. Okay?'

She swallowed and nodded, but that wasn't enough.

'Okay?' he said again.

'Yes,' she shouted back. Why the hell didn't he get on with it? If they both lived through this they could count themselves lucky.

'Right.' Max braced himself and so did she, taking two good handholds, swinging with him, to within about a foot of the oil, once ... twice ... and there was the weight of the valve giving them more momentum now ... *Three times*—Samantha gritted her teeth, screwed up her eyes, turned her head away—and heaved.

But the valve was alive, bucking crazily, and there was oil squirting everywhere, then the thing swung back and caught her off balance, her foot slipped in the oil and she was sprawling over.

'I'm all right,' she shouted across to Max as he fought to stop the valve swinging back to her. 'It just took me by surprise—I'll be fine next time,' but he gave her a minute to get her breath, and she stood bowed over, hands resting on her knees, staring down at her boots ... 'Okay,' she said, taking a deep breath. 'Let's go again,' and this time she was ready for the almighty kick, and they didn't let the valve bounce back, but managed to heave it through, even though one side of it was momentarily forced a couple of feet higher. There was oil everywhere, black, stinking stuff making everything slippery. She had closed her eyes again and couldn't see a thing, and if it caught fire now they were both done for ...

It was through. She opened her eyes in amazement, still hanging on to her side, and saw the evil jet still shooting up, but now completely encircled by the valve. She let out a low whistle. Max raised his arm again and the men slowly lowered the valve and she had to help Max manipulate it into exactly the right place.

'That's it.' His eyes shone white in a black, oily face. 'The rest I can do alone. Get the hell out of here!' and in the second she hesitated, he snarled, showing a row of glistening teeth. 'I *said* get out of here; right now I have all the problems I can handle!' and she didn't stay to hear more, but somehow slipped and staggered her way down to the ground.

Someone patted her on the shoulder with a 'Well done', then put a glass of milk in her hand. 'Get that down you—all of it,' he said, then added, 'Don't worry—he'll be all right,' and she suddenly realised it was John.

'Doesn't look as if you'll get your pure sample,' she joked almost hysterically.

'You win a few and you lose a few,' he shrugged. 'Now, drink that milk. God knows how much of that evil stuff you must have swallowed.'

So she did. All of it. But then she handed back the glass, wandered over behind a Portakabin, and was promptly sick. Then she realised she was still inside her slickers, and she pulled off the hood and tore at the fastenings at her throat. She was ringing wet inside, she could feel the perspiration running down her back. For a second she leaned against the wall breathing deeply, staring up at the burning sky and wanting to shout, 'Go away—don't you ever stop?' But then she pulled herself together and dragged her feet back to the others before she was missed, and everyone was just hanging around, standing well clear of the rig, of course, and shielding their eyes from the sun as they stared upwards, seeing if they could make out what Max was doing.

There was a clanging noise now, sounding as if he was hammering something metal. How could he stand to be up there so long—all by himself? Someone said why didn't she take off her slickers, but she shook her head, swinging her hard hat from hand to hand. If Max wanted her up there again, then she was going to be ready.

The sun, at last, began to go down, but it was still stinking hot, and everyone was working like mad to make up the thousands of gallons of mud, so that if— no, *when*, Max cut off the flow, they could get the mud down there and stabilise it. If she had only listened to him! But what was the use of 'if only'? It must be four hours now since he had started his plan. Surely he should be attempting to shut the thing off soon. But supposing the valve didn't hold? Supposing the whole lot shot off and took Max with it? What help could she be then? In desperate frustration, she peeled off the evil, smelly slickers and left them outside, before going into Frank's office and pinching a can of his Coke. She was still filthy round the edges and made sure she didn't touch anything.

'Caught you.' said John, coming in and flopping down in a chair. 'Where's Frank?'

Samantha shrugged. 'Seeing how the mud's going, I think.'

'Pete's just arrived. Say, throw us over one of those cans,' but then seeing the state of her hands, he came across and got one for himself. 'I sure as hell hope we can get those generators running soon.'

'Did he, this Pete, did he look—okay?' asked Samantha, trying not to sound anxious. She had heard about this man who was a whizz-kid with tricky mud formulas.

'You know the experts,' John tried to joke, 'everything under control.'

'Except the flipping well,' she said tetchily, and John decided not to comment on that.

'I suppose I'd better go and find him,' she said. 'He'll want to know what we've got down there . . .' But she broke off as John put up his hand.

'Do you hear that?'

'Hear what?' She strained her ears.

'Nothing! It's stopped!' John shouted, leaping up. 'He's bloody done it!' and they both raced outside, practically falling over each other down the steps. And he was right—it had gone. Only the slowly reddening evening sky could be seen through the rig's tall superstructure.

Max had done it. He'd *done* it! For a moment longer there was silence—then suddenly a cheer went up, and then another—and somehow Samantha was hugging John and now he was as black as herself, but she didn't care. Max was all right. But why didn't he come down? What was going on up there? Maybe he needed her. But then she saw the big American driller climbing up the ladder. He was the one with Yogi Bear on his hat; she guessed he couldn't wait to get it all under his control again up there.

And no, they didn't need her—silly thought. Except Pete, of course, who came marching back with Frank, wanting to go over the figures with her. But he quickly took stock and went straight back to his precious mud.

'I'm going back to town,' said John, putting his head round her office door. 'No sense in hanging on now, for either of us. There's a truck going back in a few minutes—want a lift?'

'Yes.' Samantha knew she had to get out of here fast. She wasn't needed. She was superfluous. All this was her fault, and now Max had coped with the first crisis she didn't dare think what he would have to say to her. The image of their blissful weekend—or maybe something longer together—drifted away for ever. 'Just give me five minutes to tell Frank and get my things.'

She did it in four, scooping up the oily things she had left outside and stuffing them in her cupboard with half a promise to clean them up later. If there *was* a later. Then she flung her things into the roll-bag and raced across to Frank's office.

'There's nothing I can do, is there?' she said, when he looked blank. 'I've just been offered a lift into town.'

'Yeah, yeah,' he understood at last, waving her away with an impatient hand. 'Go and get a good night's sleep. But be here first thing in the morning. Early,' he emphasised. '*Very* early,' and with these words of encouragement, Samantha fled.

She wasn't sure if she was coming back at all. Perhaps in the cool—or rather, cooler—light of morning, Frank wouldn't want her back either.

There was still no sign of Max. The Gulf Services truck was still parked behind the canteen, with all the others. Oh, there was John, waving to her, and she ran across and climbed in, squeezing in beside him and the driver who turned and grinned at her, and said, 'Welcome aboard, Hot Lips.'

It was only then that she realised she was still wearing her yellow hard hat. She took it off, managing to laugh, passing a hand across her face and getting a shock to discover how filthy she was . . .

The truck started up—she prayed it had a good air-conditioning. Now the driver was reversing around some oil drums and a pile of chain. 'First time I've seen a blow-out,' he said, in an interesting Scots burr. 'Quite something. Good thing we had Kramer with us,' which was the same, thought Samantha, as saying, 'It made up for being landed with you.'

She settled back wretchedly and closed her eyes. It wasn't necessary for him to tell her how much she had failed. And even worse—she had put Max's life in great danger.

There was no room in her mind for anything else.

CHAPTER TEN

'WHAT the hell do you mean by running out on me?' Max stormed into the hall and Samantha stepped back hurriedly. If she had known it was him she wouldn't have gone to the door. He looked dreadful; he was still wearing the jeans and bush-style shirt from this morning. He could have done with a hot bath and a stiff drink, but didn't appear to be in the mood for either.

'And what do you mean by bursting in here at this time of night?'

'It's only nine o'clock.' He brushed past her and she marched after him into the sitting room. Oh, this was all just a bit too much! She had been home barely an hour, and had only had time to shower and wonder what she was going to have for supper. Not that she felt like anything; she felt sick—upset—and there was no one to talk to . . .

'It may be only nine o'clock, but it's been a long day, and don't sit down there,' she said, when he seemed about to flop down on the settee. 'Have you seen the colour of your jeans?'

He looked cross with himself for a moment, instead of her. 'You still haven't answered me,' he said, brown eyes hard on her. 'Why did you run out on me?' And she could have screamed with frustration—he had no right to barge in here!

'I'm not needed any more, am I?' she practically screamed. 'And I didn't run out—Frank knows where I am.'

'And you didn't see fit to see me first.'

'I work for Mepco, remember?'

Max passed unsteady hands through his tumbled hair. 'Sounds like the lady's moping. What did you expect?' he taunted, 'an easy ride? Did you expect to go through this business without accidents happening? Did you expect to be carried?' He was breathing heavily, watching her intently as her face changed colour. What was he doing in Dubai anyway? . . . 'You told me once that if I didn't like the heat of this business, then I should stay out of the kitchen. Well, that's what I'm telling you now.' He strode across the room and grabbed her by the shoulders. 'Accidents happen, like I said—and they have to be dealt with. So,' he shrugged, 'today you coped. So where's the big deal? Why run out as soon as the going gets tough?'

'Let me go! How dare you!' She broke away, turning from him so that he shouldn't see the tears sparkling in her weary eyes. Didn't the brute have any sensitivity? Couldn't he tell how dreadful, how responsible, she felt about all this? But she mustn't cry—she *mustn't*. This was a man's world and she would have to learn to be as tough as them.

'But it wasn't an accident, was it?' she rounded on him. 'You warned us all what could happen.'

So,' he said, 'it *did* happen. Have you any idea of the odds against?'

'What the devil's that got to do with it?' she replied.

'Because you had every chance of being right,' he said, taking her by the shoulders again and giving her a little shake. 'You could have had some clean samples—and pretty quickly. But this time luck was stacked against you.'

'Luck!'

'Yeah—*luck!*' he repeated savagely. 'And if we hadn't had a good share of luck back there today, you and I wouldn't be standing here now.' And as they stared at each other, sharing the moment as only the two of them could, the colour drained from his face and he looked utterly desolate; astounding her by walking away across the room, then coming back and offering her his hand. 'I hope to God I never have to do that again,' he muttered, grasping her hand as she offered it, and pulling her firmly against him. And gradually it dawned on her that this was why he had come. He was as much screwed up with it all as she. He wanted to talk, he wanted reassurance as well. It was a startling discovery.

'You did a terrific job,' she began, but he wasn't listening.

'You could have been killed,' he said hopelessly. 'Killed.' Samantha wanted to look up at him, but he held her too tightly for that.

'Well, at least we wouldn't have known anything about it,' she tried to smile.

'Don't say that.' He broke away, pacing about restlessly, the tension still eating him up. 'I didn't want to, Sam. I didn't want to ask you. But there was no one else,' he insisted. 'You were the Company's engineer. It was your job.'

'I know,' she said quietly, but her stomach gave a great churn. Had Max really come to terms with her chosen career at last?

'But I swore I'd never . . .' He broke off impatiently. 'I never dreamt . . . Thank God no one was hurt,' he said after a moment, still gazing at her and looking a bit dazed—still a bit shell-shocked. 'You were great, you know. Great,' he muttered, and it was like a ton weight lifting off her shoulders. At last it was sinking in that he wasn't blaming her. That no one seemed to be blaming her. And he wasn't accusing anyone else either. It was an accident.

'Would you like some supper?' she asked, suddenly feeling terribly hungry, and terribly, terribly tired.

'What?' He took a minute to come back to her. 'Yes, that would be fine.' But he still wandered about looking as if he didn't know what to do, or what to say. He followed her through to the kitchen and watched as she began rummaging in the fridge. 'I guess I could use a shower—or two—or three,' he said, glancing down at himself with disgust. 'You must have been mad to let me in here—I look a freak,' he grinned, and that was better. That was more like Max. Her Max.

'Help yourself,' she said, aware that the atmosphere was subtly changing. 'But I don't have anything else for you to put on.'

'I've got my bag outside in the car—everything I need.'

While he showered she put all the available food on the table; there wasn't much. 'Would toasted sausage sandwiches be all right?' she asked doubtfully, and he said toasted sausage sandwiches sounded just great.

They were.

'Let's take the coffee through to the other room,' she said, when they had eaten their way through a pound of sausages and three-quarters of a loaf. 'I think there are some apples in there.' And when the coffee was ready she brought it through on a tray and sat down on the settee beside him as he invitingly patted the seat.

'This is a perfect end to a—not very perfect day,' he said, sliding an arm around her shoulders and drawing her back against him.

Samantha relaxed with a deep sigh. How good he felt! 'I've just remembered,' she began contentedly. 'I got my drinks licence while you were away and stocked up with booze. Would you like a brandy with that?'

'Does it mean you have to get up?' he murmured sleepily, his thumb slowly caressing her arm.

Samantha measured the distance out into the

kitchen with her eye. 'I rather think it does,' she admitted.

'Then I think I'd rather go without,' which suited her fine too, because this was really too cosy to move away from and the sound of his deep, deep breathing was having an hypnotic effect on her . . .

Moments later she realised he had fallen asleep, and she managed to get the coffee mug out of his hand without waking him up. Moving carefully, she leaned forward and put it on the low table. Her eyes never left him. It was late. Would it really matter if he spent the night on the settee? Settee? Who was she kidding?

Afraid of waking him, she managed to slip out of his grasp and slide on to the floor, cradling her knees and smiling up at him. What a crazy day! And then she allowed herself the exquisite pleasure of studying him in intimate detail. His hair had dried now, but it was still tousled and twisted, flicking round his ears— teasing across a temple, contrasting sharply with the glowing bronze of his skin. His face was relaxed now, the forehead smooth, but there was still a little crease between his eyes, as if he had been staring into the sun for a long time. Everything about this man spoke of the out of doors, she thought dreamily. A man used to fighting nature—a man used to winning . . . Her eyes travelled down the broad span of his chest; he was wearing a loose blue track suit top, but it didn't hide the lethal strength lying dormant beneath.

For a moment she had to fight an irresistible urge to go back to him, to kiss him awake—to smooth her hands across his body . . .

His legs were splayed out in the abandoned attitude of sleep. They stretched underneath the coffee table; long legs, iron-hard. For a moment her eyes were rooted to the dangerous curve of muscular thighs accentuated by his clean white jeans.

He had shaved—she had noticed that the minute he had sat down for supper. And she smiled to herself again, remembering the peace that had descended over them—the rightness of him being there.

It was at that moment that Samantha knew she didn't want Max to leave tonight.

Feeling suddenly jittery, and wanting something to do, she took the mugs back into the kitchen and quietly began clearing up.

'You're not going to wash up now,' said Max, coming over behind her at the sink, and she was so surprised she nearly dropped a plate. He chuckled softly, turning her round in his arms and lowering his head to kiss her. 'I think this is a much better idea, don't you?' he whispered, as she moaned against him. And it all began as easily as that; a kiss in the kitchen, a slow languorous kiss that had them melting into each other, had them sliding firm, demanding hands down each other's back until they were moving, breathing, *existing* as one being. 'It's late,' he murmured, when all her limbs had turned to water.

'I know.' She nibbled his ear.

'I ought to go home,' he tried again.

She didn't reply.

'You've had a very tough day.' His voice was deep, husky, sensual, and as she wriggled longingly, she felt the tension in him begin to string together. 'If we carry on like this, you know where we'll end up?'

'Mmm . . . ' was all she could think to say.

Max eased her from him, suddenly looking awfully smug. 'And what about our weekend—the big fling?'

'Couldn't we have that as well?' she suggested, peeping up at him with eyes that were infinitely wicked.

'You little . . . ' he breathed, and he was scooping her into his arms, manoeuvring her into the passageway, then he hesitated, laughing, and asked. 'Which room's yours?'

She told him. Only it was a bit difficult when they got inside, and she had switched on the lamp beside the bed, because now the laughing had stopped—Max was suddenly very, very serious, and as he reached for the tie of her wrap she knew that from now on there would be no turning back.

The belt came undone easily, and the soft, silky material fell apart, giving him the first glimpse of her naked body underneath.

'Beautiful,' he breathed, parting the fronts with a gentle finger, bending down to kiss her breasts, her stomach . . . and she closed her eyes as the blood began hammering through her veins. This was madness—*madness*. She was out of her mind. He thought she was experienced . . .

'I—just have to go the bathroom,' she said, in a stifled panic, but that wasn't much of an excuse because in a minute she would have to come out again.

But she cleaned her teeth and stared at herself in the mirror. Samantha Whittaker, you're mad. You can't go through with it. But that was only fooling herself, because Max Kramer was out there waiting for her, and he was the most devastating, the most exciting man she had ever met. And she knew it would be utterly impossible to feel like this about anyone else, ever again. She loved him. Very much. And he had come here tonight because he had wanted to be with her. Not to go to bed—not then, he had been too shattered, too worked up with the day to have been thinking about that. But he had wanted to talk. It was almost as if he knew how desperately she had wanted to talk as well. And hadn't he driven thirty miles back through the desert after the toughest kind of day a man could have? Would he have done that unless he *cared*?

Samantha took a deep breath and unlocked the door. Max was already in bed waiting for her. As she crossed the room to join him she knew that before the sun shone again she would be a totally different person.

'Cold?' Max sounded surprised as she quickly slipped off her robe and slid between her sheets. 'Or is it nerves?' he joked, not really meaning it. And then with a certain concern, he added, 'Has it been—quite some time? . . .'

'Er—yes,' she muttered, which would make him gentle, wouldn't it? And she gasped as an arm snaked round her and pulled her down to meet him. This time she shivered with delight as bare skin made contact with bare skin.

'Nice,' he taunted, his dark shadow covering her, his strong, muscled body smooth, hard, infinitely exciting, and she found herself arching urgently towards him—suddenly desperate . . . 'Shh . . .' he whispered. 'Not yet.' And now he was sliding off her and smiling when she groaned. Then he began kissing her, tiny, tiny kisses that covered her face, her neck, and lingered on the erratic pulse in her throat.

'Max,' she managed to breathe at last as his lips moved down to the tip of her breast. 'Oh—that's lovely,' and she gave another little cry of delight as deep warm waves of desire began flooding through her body. She took a deep breath and held on to it tightly, her hands strong on his neck, holding him there— never wanting him to stop—and all the while his searching hand was travelling dangerously down her body, coaxing, caressing, intimately possessive . . .

This wasn't real. This couldn't possibly be happening. After all the arguments, after all the battles of will, could she possibly be sharing her bed with Max? It couldn't be Max making love to her. But it was. And it felt so *right*. She wasn't feeling ashamed— not even shy. But perhaps she was still a bit scared . . .

'What's the matter, darling?' His voice was soft yet

gravelly, as he lifted his head and smiled down at her with misty brown eyes.

'N-nothing,' she breathed, reaching up to smooth the strong line of his cheek, and he captured her hand and kissed it, then rolled back on to the pillow, pulling her over on top of him.

For a moment she panicked. Now it was her turn and he would expect her to know exactly how to please him. Should she tell him now? Should she explain that she hadn't gone this far before? But instead of speaking, Samantha found herself bending to kiss his lips; slowly, provocatively, sliding her naked body over his ... Teasing him by pretending she was stopping ... Then beginning again when he started to protest. And all the while the lines of tension were building up in the tautness of his face. She could feel the latent power stirring inside him ...

She could do it. It was easy. With joy and confidence surging inside her, she abandoned herself; touching, kissing, caressing ... exploring, revelling in the long length of his naked magnificence. And the more she pleased him the more she pleased herself, until in an agony of pent-up longing, she bit him none too gently on the thigh.

'Minx!' he roared, reaching down for her, tossing her on to her back amidst the pillows. 'That's what you want, is it? A fight?' And then they were all arms and legs, struggling, laughing. But his gentle mood had passed. As her hands ran firm and strong down his back, she could feel all the bunched up sexual aggression, all the life and dangerous vitality of the man. And he was using his strength now, fighting and rolling, but all the while remorselessly forcing her to submit. And it was so exciting, so *exciting* ... He was nudging the inside of her thighs, pinning her arms over her head, holding her wrists together with one hand, and as she wriggled and bucked his smouldering eyes were all over her, loving what she was doing—convinced she knew the game she was playing—and all the rules!

'I think we've waited long enough,' he breathed raggedly, his free hand thrusting beneath her—drawing her towards him . . .

'Max!' she cried out in panic, because he didn't know, and in *this* mood . . . But he misread her plea, coming down hard on top of her; the sudden pain froze the cry on her lips as her whole body went rigid.

'Oh, my God!' Max released her arms immediately, taking his own weight on his elbows. He didn't move an inch—he didn't even breathe . . .

Samantha opened her eyes, surprised that the lashes were wet with tears, and he burrowed his taut face into her neck.

'Why didn't you tell me?' he said after a moment, when he had forced a relaxed smile on his face. 'Hmm—why didn't you?' and he gently smoothed a few wayward curls off her cheek.

'I don't know,' she muttered, feeling an awful fool now, dreadfully embarrassed—and scared to move.

'Relax.' He kissed the tip of her nose. 'I didn't know—I . . .' His face creased in agony. 'I thought you wanted me to be rough.'

'I know. Look, it doesn't matter. It doesn't hurt any more.'

'Doesn't it?' he whispered.

She shook her head.

He moved gently against her and she automatically held her breath. 'Ssh,' he said softly, 'relax . . . think of something nice . . .' That made her giggle and she discovered it was impossible to giggle and remain tense. 'Better?' he tried again, bending to kiss her lips, beginning to caress her soft, rounded breast, and all the while those lethal, narrow hips began a gentle, gentle rhythm of their own.

Slowly, gradually, pleasure crossed Samantha's face.
There was no pain now, in fact . . . 'Oh . . .' How silly
she had been, how stupid to have felt suddenly afraid.
But all that had gone now and her world was full of
Max making love to her—taking his time—waiting for
her instinctive reactions which soon came. And then
she was moving with him, revelling in the voluptuous,
sensuous abandonment of spirit—of self . . . On and
on, cradled in his arms, gently moving as one, until
they became one . . . And then at long, long last his
patience was rewarded as her fingers squeezed into his
shoulders, and the warm, deep heat began fluttering
inside her, getting stronger—longer . . . Until she was
engulfed completely, crying out, clutching him tightly
against her as the exquisite agony exploded all the way
down to her toes. She heard Max cry out and for a
second her body was raked by the thundering intimacy
of his possession . . . And then he folded himself on
top of her, his face nestling against hers on the pillow,
and all she could do was to lie beneath him, trying to
drag herself back, her limbs drugged heavy with
passion. She tried to stretch down and pull the sheet
over his damp back. But she couldn't find it—and her
eyelids were so heavy—so heavy . . .

Samantha woke to the gentle hum of the air-conditioning. For a moment wondering why she felt so
excited—why different? And then it all came back
and she turned her head . . . And there was Max, flat out
on his back, taking up three-quarters of the bed, the
sheet covering him up to the waist. The strength and
breadth of his chest covered by a smattering of dark
auburn hair made her fingers itch to caress him.

Then she automatically turned to see what time it
was. Oh no—not already! But before she could jump
up, a strong arm snaked round her waist and Max was
rolling her over towards him.

'We have to get up—now,' she moaned, and then as her eyes widened wickedly, 'Don't do that!'

'Aren't you going to give me a good morning kiss?' said Max, reaching up for her and looking dangerously predatory.

She kissed him briefly, fighting the desire to linger. 'It's nearly seven o'clock. Frank wants me out at the rig early . . .' She broke off as his face momentarily darkened.

'Be late,' he challenged. 'Tell me how much you enjoyed last night.'

'I can't,' she pleaded. Not to save time, but because she was suddenly shy.

'Try,' he persisted, and she realised this was important to him. Come to that, important to them both. More important than being out at the rig on time? But she pushed the idea way.

'All right,' she agreed, pulling the sheet right over their heads, and he laughed and tickled her, and the awkward little moment passed.

'Last night was wonderful,' he said, when they had calmed down and she was lying in his arms. 'Wonderful for me, anyway,' he added dryly. And then, smoothing her cheek, he added, 'How—do you feel this morning?'

Samantha knew exactly what he meant, but wasn't prepared to admit her aches and pains to anyone. Instead she propped herself up on her elbows and smiled down into the familiar, intimate warmth of his welcoming eyes. At this minute she couldn't imagine loving anyone half as much. But she mustn't start clinging—or making him feel responsible. This was to be a relationship on equal terms. But he looked more serious than she had expected. Was that his way of warning her not to get too close?

She kissed him, then gave a bright, cheerful smile, forcing herself to lighten the atmosphere, aware that unconsciously his firm hand was smoothing her bottom. 'If I'd told you, last night, about being a virgin—would it have stopped you?' and her tone implied that she was laughing at herself.

Max gaxed up at her, his eyes and face enigmatic—serious. 'Of course it would have stopped me,' he said quietly. 'I'd have waited for our weekend . . . spent all night and all day with you . . .' And she bowed her head and kissed his shoulder quickly, because she suddenly felt rather small.

'Thank you,' she mumbled, then looking up with a wicked grin, 'but I'm very glad you didn't know—and you didn't wait . . .'

'You mean that?' he said huskily, and when she nodded, he pulled her down on top of him again, and slowly, slowly, the magic began all over again.

'We can't,' Samantha moaned. 'Darling Max, there isn't time . . .' But then she forgot the time—and so did he—as once again they made love. And this time she noted a new possessiveness in the touch of his lips, she noted a proprietorial awakening of her senses and an urgent possession of her body, that had her crying, dying . . . forgetting the world existed for more than the two of them . . .

'Lie there,' Max muttered drowsily, how much longer afterwards she couldn't be sure. 'I'll go and put the kettle on,' and as he reluctantly moved away from her, he added, 'Tea or coffee?'

A slow, fat smile spread across Samantha's face.

'What's so funny?' he asked, glad to have the excuse to linger, running a caressing hand along the inside of her thigh.

She shivered with delight. '*You're* funny,' she said at last, opening her eyes, and the sudden sight of him bending over her, smiling, made a great stab of pain twist in her stomach. Lord, how she loved him. How would she live when he had finished with her? She pushed the thought aside. 'We spend the night together,' she explained, 'and in the morning you have to ask whether I drink tea or coffee. It's funny, that's all,' and she knew that really he had understood all the time.

'Tell me, then?' he grinned.

She told him, and while he went to make the tea, she somehow dragged herself out of bed and stumbled into the shower. Ten minutes and she was in the kitchen wearing clean jeans and tee-shirt and with a headful of soaking curls.

She found some eggs, that had hidden in the fridge last night, and started feeding bread into the toaster. Max went to dress, and when he came back breakfast was ready, but he was looking serious again. Was he expecting her to become weepy?

'I wonder how they're getting on—at the rig,' she added, when he frowned. 'We're going to be ever so late. Frank will probably never speak to me again . . .' But she broke off as Max's eyes flashed angrily across the table.

'About last night,' he said, taking a steadying breath, picking up his fork and chasing the scrambled egg around the plate.

Samantha's heart sank. It was suddenly difficult to swallow. He was going to back off now—make some trite remark about this being the twentieth century.

'It was great,' she said brightly. 'We must do it again some day,' but that seemed to be the final straw, because he clattered down his fork, scraped back his chair, and marched round to her side of the table.

'Is that all it means to you? Is that all *I* mean to you?' And as he grasped her arms and actually lifted her to her feet, her chair fell over and crashed to the floor.

'I don't know what you mean,' she began, appalled at his anger when she wanted, *needed*, his gentleness. 'What else do you want me to say?'

'Like maybe you——' but he broke off, letting her go and turning to pick up the chair.

'Isn't that what you normally say?' she retaliated. '*Wouldn't* it be nice to do it again?'

'Oh, sure.' He paced over to the sink and back again. 'When do you fancy? Tomorrow? Next week? Next month . . .? Oh, but no, you won't be here next month, will you?' he added savagely. 'Don't let me forget that you petroleum engineers only work for twenty-eight consecutive days. Then you'll be darting back to England . . .'

So he had gone off the idea of her moving in with him. 'I really don't see why you should throw my job up into my face, *now* of all times,' she said angrily. 'I only meant that I wanted to see you again.' But she would have done better to keep quiet.

'My God, how cool!' His eyes darkened as he marched up to her, possessive hands running up and down her arms until he caught hold of one of her wrists. 'Are you sure it was your first time last night?' And she put all her weight behind her free hand and slapped him hard across the face.

A line around his lips turned white and all the old rage was boiling away inside him.

Samantha broke away, turning from him so that he shouldn't see the tears in her eyes. Nothing had changed. Nothing had changed. She and Max were still antagonists.

One night. That was all she would have to remember.

CHAPTER ELEVEN

'Max—I'm sorry,' Samantha stumbled, glancing back in desperation, and suddenly appalled to see him still staring into space. 'I shouldn't have done that.'

He blinked and took a deep breath. 'Yes, you should. I deserved it.' He came across to her quickly, taking her hands, folding her into his arms. 'Why do we always end up fighting?' he said sadly. 'I love you, Samantha. I *love* you,' and with a gentle finger under her chin, he persuaded her to look up at him. 'And I want you to marry me. I want that very much.' And his eyes were wide, searching, attempting to see into her mind for her answer, willing her to say, 'Yes.'

'I—I don't know.' Uncertainties whizzed around her mind. 'It's a bit sudden. We've only known each other a fortnight. What—what about the others?'

'Others?' He smiled, but his face was a bit tight.

'Jessica—Farida . . .'

His expression became more strained. 'Jessica and I have an—arrangement,' he began warily. 'But there are no strings—no commitment—we're both free to go our own way. And you know about Farida,' he said, brightening. 'She belongs to someone else.'

'I know she does—technically, I know you're not engaged, but I thought . . .'

'Thought what?' His eyes were quietly grave.

'Thought that you and she had a—an arrangement as well.'

He grinned sideway. 'Not for quite a while.'

'But she was at your bungalow the other night waiting for you to get back from Bahrain. I know she was there—I phoned you quite late . . .'

'Did you now? . . .' He was looking rather pleased with himself.

'About the stem-testing,' she added, and his face dropped. 'Well? What was she doing there if she wasn't . . .?'

'Staying with Sue-Lee. I told you,' he explained. 'I don't like leaving the kid alone. Farida's been very kind. She was a friend of Lee's parents—that's how I met her. When I'm away sometimes Farida comes over to stay with Lee—and sometimes Lee goes over to stay with her—like now.'

'Oh.' Samantha turned away. Funny, she could accept that the 'bright lights' Jessica was no more than a passing fancy. But Farida was different, she was positive Max felt deeply for her. And then she remembered the evening in Frank's office when she and Max had got back from the sandstorm . . . 'You seemed pretty upset, last week—when we got back from the rig and Frank told you Farida had cancelled your date. That doesn't seem to make your relationship very much in the past.'

Max took a deep breath, forcing himself to relax. It was pretty obvious, even in these circumstances, that he didn't like being cross-questioned.

'Upset isn't the right word,' he began. 'I was sorry—concerned. She'd phoned me the day before about a letter she had received from her parents . . .'

'About getting married?' Samantha interrupted.

'Yes. She's known for some time that she had to come to a decision sooner or later. She was worried. She wanted to talk to me about it. When Frank Douglas told me she couldn't keep our date,' he shrugged, 'I was worried for her. Sorry she wouldn't be able to have a long talk about it that night.'

'You must still be very close, then,' she said, when his explanation seemed to have come to an end.

'Yes—as friends. She's been a tremendous help with

Lee—I couldn't have agreed to Lee staying with me, if Farida hadn't offered to help.' And from the look in her eyes he realised that Samantha wanted to know about why Lee was living with him. 'I told you Lee's father was killed on that Mepco rig. Well, her mother remarried this summer—the new husband lives in Hongkong—and Lee didn't want to go over there ... She's jealous of her stepfather. It's understandable. It'll take time.'

'And meanwhile she stays with you?' said Samantha, amazed that he had committed himself to that kind of responsibility.

He shrugged. 'For as long as it takes. The kid's at a difficult age. She goes to a good school here—it seemed a pity to break everything up ...' Then his lips twisted and she knew he was about to tease her. 'So you see the dilemma I'm in. Farida disappearing back to Syria. Lee needs a woman about. I'm forced to think about getting married ...'

'Wretch!' she laughed, looking round for a tea-towel to throw at him.

'Come on,' he cajoled, pulling her lightly into his arms again, and kissing the top of her wet curls. 'Am I such a bad proposition? Think of it,' he taunted, 'nights like last night—days of being together. No more work, no more stinking heat ...' He broke off as Samantha wriggled out of his arms.

'You mean—you'd want me to give up work?' she said, with a bit of a croak.

'But there'd be no need, darling.' Max spread his hands persuasively. 'We certainly don't need the money—you must realise that. And the hours I work, the kind of life I lead—well, you know what the oil business is like ... When I get home I'd need you there. I'd want us to be together. And no sane man would want his wife working out there in those conditions—wondering what's happening—

wondering what situation she was getting herself into . . .'

'But I couldn't just give up working,' she said hopelessly. 'I mean . . .'

'I'm not suggesting that you give up *work*,' he said eagerly, giving her his most disarming smile. 'But, darling, there are lots of other things you can do here in town; jobs with sensible hours which would give us time to be together . . .' but he broke off as Samantha screwed up her hands and turned away.

And that was when she saw her hard hat, still sitting on the work surface where she had dumped it after coming in from the rig last night. She went over and smoothed it with possessive fingers, smiling tearfully at the saucy stickers. It had taken her a long time to earn it; years of study, long hard hours of work. And it was her job—her identity. It was as much a part of her as Max's career was to him. *She* wouldn't have dreamed of asking him to give up his job. What right had he to ask her to give up hers? If she wasn't always there when he got back home, what about all the days—weeks—when he could be flying off anywhere in the Middle East—how was she supposed to do without him?

She put the hat back on the counter. 'I—I don't think I can marry you in those circumstances,' she said in an icy whisper, while inside her heart was crying out, pleading with him to love her enough to understand . . .

His face tightened and a muscle jerked in his cheek. 'That's your final word?'

'My job's important to me.' She started digging her fingernails into the palms of her hands.

He smiled weakly. Did he think he was making it easy for her? 'Then I suppose I'd better leave,' he said, but seemed unable to budge from the spot.

'I suppose so,' Samantha swallowed awkwardly. If he didn't leave soon she would break down and cry.

'I'll just get my things,' and she remained motionless while he went through to the bedroom and gathered his bits and pieces. A minute later he was back, but still seemed to be looking round for an excuse to linger. Why didn't he just *get out*! 'Sorry about breakfast,' he began.

She glanced at the uneaten food and shrugged.

'And I'm very sorry about—everything.' He gave a strange little cough.

'So am I,' she said, still staring at the floor, pretty certain now that her palms were beginning to bleed.

As she glanced at him at last, he nodded vaguely, tightened his face even harder, then abruptly turned away and went out of the back door.

At last Samantha let out a long, shuddering sigh, slid down the table and doubled up on the floor, hugging her knees in an attempt at comfort, slowly uncoiling her hands ... Four little red half-moons stared up at her. But the pain they brought was nothing compared to the pain deep inside, splitting her in two, as she heard Max's car starting up and then the sound of screeching tyres as he roared back down her drive and into the little lane, in screaming reverse.

For a full minute she screwed herself up tight and hung on like mad ... and then, stiff, and strangely old, she slowly clambered to her feet and began automatically clearing the table.

Max couldn't have driven more than half a mile when there was the noise of footsteps outside, the back door suddenly burst open and he was standing there again—bringing the heat of the morning in with him.

'I'm stuck,' he said angrily, as if this was just too much on top of everything else. 'I reversed into the lane, but my foot slipped on the accelerator and I shot all the way down to the beach.'

Samantha made a big effort to pull herself together. Thank heaven she had forced herself not to cry. 'Can't you drive it out?' Wasn't he a wizard when it came to driving on sand?

'I've got the Chev, not the Range Rover.' He scraped back his thick wavy hair. 'Look—I'm sorry, Samantha, would you mind if I—phone a garage?'

'No. No—I mean, *I'll* do it,' she said quickly, indicating that he should stay in the kitchen while she hurried into the sitting room. It was a strange sensation, as if it had all happened before. But last time it had been the other way around. Last time she had been stuck in the sand and he had phoned a garage—only they hadn't come, had they?

She flicked through the phone book quickly. Could she do it? Dare she? Was there any point? But Max was actually *back here in her kitchen*. And she had never thought even to see him again. Didn't her love mean anything? Didn't she owe herself—owe them both—the chance to try again? She picked up the phone, punched out any old number rapidly, then making sure he wasn't coming, she put her finger firmly over the button.

'They said they won't be long,' she lied, coming back into the kitchen, and scraping off the cold scrambled egg into the bin.

He nodded, as if he didn't trust himself to speak, and watched hawk-eyed as she carried on clearing the table.

'You're going straight out there—to the rig?' he said tightly. 'I'm holding you up?'

She shrugged. 'It doesn't matter,' and inwardly added, 'Let them wait!'

It was dreadful. She could only make the washing up last so long, even with the last night's things there wasn't very much. And behind her Max was pacing about, back and forth . . . back and forth. He kept glancing at the clock. And then at his watch . . . and it was even worse for her because she knew definitely that no one was coming. Then it suddenly occurred to her that perhaps her car would tow him out. But she would pretend she hadn't thought of that. Actually, it was surprising *he* hadn't thought of it.

'They're taking their time,' Max tried again, and as she glanced over her shoulder he looked quickly away.

'I don't suppose they'll be long,' she said. 'Perhaps they're having trouble finding the place. All these bungalows look alike.'

'Mmm . . .' He began drumming his fingers on the table. 'Look, I'm sorry, Sam,' and her heart missed a beat. 'I mean—coming back, like this. I know it's awkward.'

Desperately she tried to think of something besides the inane, 'Yes.'

'I don't know what got into me,' Max was struggling on, and she realised she had never seen him struggle before—not even out on the rig. 'The car just shot back. Thank God there was no one in the way.' Then he paced over to the door . . . and back again.

'I don't suppose they'll be long now.' Lord, that was the second time she'd said that.

'If you want to leave, go ahead. I'll—I'll wait for them outside.'

'No. No, it's all right,' she said quickly. 'I was just going—er—to make some coffee. Would you? . . .' He nodded and she filled the kettle. Better make instant, he might think there shouldn't be time for anything else. They didn't speak again until she slid the mug across the table, and when she perched on the edge of one of the chairs, he did the same.

'This is crazy,' he said, after a few minutes, when Samantha had decided her nerves had been stretched to breaking point. 'After last night—we shouldn't be sitting here like this.'

'No,' she agreed huskily, looking down at her coffee as tears blurred her eyes.

'I don't want to lose you, Samantha . . .' Their glances met briefly then darted away. 'But don't you see,' he continued sadly, 'I couldn't live with the uncertainty—the fear that something would happen to you.'

'*Nothing* would happen to me,' she said wearily, but at least they were talking again. She glanced quickly at the clock, almost half past eight. How long before he suggested that she phone the garage again? 'How often do you hear of bad accidents these days?'

'Often!' And this time, when their eyes met, neither of them looked away. 'Two years ago it was Sue-Lee's father on one of *Mepco's* offshore rigs,' he reminded her.

Samantha sighed. 'You can't keep on blaming them. And you can't keep on blaming Frank.'

Max made an impatient gesture with his hand. 'Frank's getting too old for this business. It's time he went back to the States.'

'He's lonely.' Samantha knew she was really offering an explanation for any extra-curricular attention she had been giving to her employer.

Max seemed to understand. 'Frank's a fool,' he said harshly, 'but I don't blame him directly for what happened to Lee's father—I blame myself.'

Samantha's green eyes widened in surprise.

'Two years ago was like a re-run of yesterday,' Max began angrily. 'Frank, Company man—me carrying out tests against my better judgment. Only that time somebody did get hurt. And that's why yesterday it could have been *you*.'

'I didn't know you'd been involved—that you were there at the time,' she said wretchedly, beginning to understand his obsession. But he shouldn't blame himself, that was dreadful. 'But you didn't have any alternative. The Company always has the final say. If Mepco wanted you to . . .'

'But I could have refused.' Max hammered his fist down on the table and some of the coffee spilled. 'I could have refused two years ago—and I could have refused yesterday . . .'

'Then why didn't you?' she interrupted, and he glared at her, realising perfectly well that she knew the answer.

'Because if *I* hadn't done the job, some other service company would have been called in to do the same thing . . .'

'And if anyone was going to do it, it was going to be you, because you're the best there is out here in the Gulf.'

'Yes. Okay,' he admitted grudgingly. 'But that's no excuse . . .'

'It's *every* excuse, don't you *see!*' she exclaimed, thumping down on the table herself. 'Two years ago you were unlucky. *Unlucky!* But yesterday it worked. If *you* hadn't been around to stab that valve we might have a real emergency on our hands. It's over, Max. Forget it. And if you think you can go round protecting the world from itself, then boy, you're fighting a losing battle!'

'But don't I have the right to protect my wife?' he came back harshly. 'Is that so much to ask?'

'Nobody has that kind of right,' she said quietly, and he could take that any way he liked.

'I don't understand you,' and he was staring at her as if he had never seen her before in his life.

'Would I have the right to make you change your job? Would I?' she persisted. '*If* we were married.'

'That's different.' He pushed back his chair and began pacing about again.

'It is *not* different!' Now she was on her feet. 'If anyone has a dangerous job, it's you. You know as much about controlling blow-outs as the experts.'

'I know no such thing.'

'Then you intend finding out, don't you? And what do you think it would be like for me, staying at home, waiting for you ... out of my mind with worry . . .?'

'You wouldn't be . . .'

'How dare you suggest that you have more feelings than me! Do you really think your wife would take your job casually when you've just admitted that you couldn't live with the uncertainty of mine?'

'I didn't mean—*of course* you'll be concerned.'

'So it's all right for me to stay at home, going grey with *concern*—as long as no one expects you to cope with the same worry!'

He stared at her, long, hard and fiercely, and then suddenly all his aggression came out in a long sigh. 'I shouldn't have come back,' he said, staring up at the ceiling. 'This is getting worse.'

Samantha flopped down on a chair again. 'Yes,' she muttered, 'but I suppose it had to be said.'

'You drive a hard bargain,' said Max, eventually looking across at her again.

'It isn't a bargain,' she said exasperatedly, and then more softly, 'But it's my life,' and although he looked momentarily uncertain, his face and lips soon set in a determined line.

'I'm not accustomed to being dictated to.' He sounded as if he didn't intend getting used to the idea, either.

'If that's what you think, then there really is nothing more to say.' Somehow Samantha found the strength to drag herself to her feet again. 'I'm not dictating, Max. Can't you see that? It would defeat the whole issue. We have to meet each other half way. You have to *believe* in what I'm saying, Max. Really believe. Otherwise we might as well say goodbye now.'

He laughed harshly. 'I thought we already had,' and for a moment there was a brief lull, an unacknowledged coming together, each waiting for the other to make the first move.

'I don't think they're coming—the garage,' he said at last.

'Do you want me to phone again?' Perhaps it would be best not to keep her finger on the button this time.

'Give them a bit longer,' he said, and the quietness ticked on, measured by the kitchen clock, and he perched on the edge of the table, crossing his arms and ankles . . . staring down at his feet. 'And if I . . . come to meet you,' he began slowly, 'how far will you come to meet me?'

'I don't see . . .' she began. 'You know I wouldn't stop you doing your work.'

'Until I get to Frank's age?' he suggested with a little grin.

'Until you get to Frank's age,' she repeated softly, sighing inside as his face hardened again.

'But life's not all work,' and the rage was back; had it ever been away? 'I want a family, Samantha. Children. *Our* children.'

'Well—and so do I,' she stammered, because she hadn't been thinking as far ahead as that. 'Eventually.'

'Oh, is that so? And how do you propose to deal with a day like yesterday if we had a family? Huh? Strap the baby on your back? Isn't that what you women do these days when you go on your marches?'

'Now you're just being ridiculous.' It was Samantha's turn to start pacing about. 'Sure I want a family in a year or two. And of course I'd have to give up work for a while . . .'

'So you agree that a kid needs a mother.'

'Yes,' she snapped. 'And a father too. But I'm telling you straight, Max, I don't intend devoting the next fifteen years of my life exclusively to nappies, cooking and the kitchen sink. If you want that kind of wife you should look elsewhere.' It occurred to her that when he had left earlier, it had been mutually agreed that he should look elsewhere, but now wasn't the time to remind him of that.

'I'm not saying you should devote your time to nappies—and whatever . . .'

'Aren't you?'

'No, Sam.' He sighed warily. He seemed to be doing a lot of that this morning. 'That doesn't sound very much like you at all.'

'Then what are we arguing about?' She tried a little smile.

'I suppose you wouldn't consider working for me?'

She was about to say, 'No', when she remembered about meeting him halfway. 'In what capacity?' she asked instead. 'I didn't think you employed petroleum engineers.'

'We don't.'

'So you mean I'd be in the office—administration?'

He shook his head. 'I'm not a fool. With your experience you'd be out in the field. Among other things—drill stem-testing . . . Which means you'd have to go away on a course, and I'd hate that, but not as much as I'd hate you carrying on working for Mepco. Sam, I couldn't cope with it. I mean it. They don't break the rules, but they take chances—too many chances. You can come in with me. Work for any other company in the Gulf . . . except maybe . . .' but he didn't go further when he saw the warning look in her eyes. 'Well,' he added roughly after a moment, 'what's it to be?'

'I'm not sure. I don't know if it would be a good idea to work together.'

'I thought that was one of your priorities. I thought we were supposed to be a team.'

Samantha shook her head and her red curls caught the sun weakly filtering through the tinted window. 'You know what I mean. We'd have to give it a lot of thought. But—well, if I *didn't* work for you . . .'

'*With* me,' Max corrected.

'Okay, but if I didn't work with you, then I'll agree to look out for another job. But I'm not going to accept just anything.'

'You won't have to. After yesterday, the whole Gulf's going to be talking about you.'

'Don't be ridiculous,' she grinned.

'I love you. And I'm very proud of you,' he said suddenly, and his eyes were dark, fathomless pools of fire.

'And I love you too . . .'

'Then come over here and kiss me quickly,' he said, holding out his hand, and suddenly the space between dissolved into nothing and she was flinging her arms around him, kissing him eagerly, her whole being singing out with a joy she hadn't dared to imagine could really exist.

Max folded her hard against him, as if he had no intention of ever letting her go, and for a while there were no words, no movement, as they clung to each other in utter, unbelievable relief.

'*Will* you marry me?' he whispered at last, and she reluctantly eased out of his tight grasp.

'Yes, please.' Her eyes and face gleamed. 'I think I'd like that very much.'

They kissed.

'Wasn't it a good thing the garage men didn't come?' Samantha teased, feeling very pleased with herself, and wondering if she dared tell him the truth.

Max grinned, then perched down on the edge of the table again and possessively trapped her between his thighs. 'Shall I let you into a little secret?' he taunted, looking pleased with himself as well. 'When I drove away from here this morning, I thought, what the hell are you doing? Only a fool runs away from a girl like that.' Did he *really* think that? Samantha was amazed. 'So do you know what I did?' he continued.

She shook her head.

'I drove straight back on to the beach. Knew I'd be stuck. Or, at least, look stuck.'

'You mean you weren't?'

He shook his head. 'But I had to get back in here somehow. Cross?'

'You know I'm not,' and she gasped as his hands slid down her back, over her bottom ... drawing her nearer. They lost the next ten minutes in a hazy dream of their own making.

'And shall I tell you something?' she said, when he eventually released her. 'When I went into the other room to phone the garage—I didn't.' She peeped at him provocatively through her lashes. 'I held the button down ...' and he laughed in a dazed, unbelieving sort of way. And then, remembering something, he began laughing all the more.

'Why are you laughing?' she asked, gazing up at the lean, strong, sunburnt face, at the magical eyes and sensuous mouth that had the power to drive her crazy ... Knowing without doubt that he would always remain in dominant mastery of her senses.

'I'm laughing at you,' he said, 'not making the call.'

'It's not *that* funny!'

He obviously thought it was. 'Remember when you were stuck in the sand and you wouldn't let me pull you out?' She nodded—how could she ever forget? 'And you came charging indoors when the garage didn't turn up ...'

'You don't mean ...?' she began disbelievingly.

'Yes, I do,' he grinned. 'I didn't make the call either.'

'But you did. You sat there and held the phone out—and I heard it ringing.'

He shook his head. 'That wasn't a garage. That was my office—my private line, not the answerphone. I knew there was no one there.'

Samantha was thunderstruck. 'I thought you remembered the number very easily.' And did that mean that, even then, he had known there was something between them? ... 'Why—why did you want to keep me there?' she whispered shyly.

'Let's say I knew I'd met a very special lady—and I wanted to see her again.'

'I'm very glad,' she said quietly, and his eyes and hands were soft and warm on her as he answered.

'So am I.'

Then for some reason Samantha glanced at the clock. 'Good heavens!' she groaned. 'And I said I'd be out there early ... Max darling ...'

'I know,' he said. 'We'll use your car. It'll be quicker than trying to get mine out.'

'I'll just go and get my things,' and she raced through to the bedroom, surprised by the tumble of unmade bedclothes, revelling in the pleasure they so easily evoked. But she didn't have time to make the bed—that would have to wait until later.

Max was still in the kitchen, holding open the door, and she charged through, grabbing sunglasses and the car keys from the windowsill. They both gave a swift glance round to see if they had forgotten anything, and it was Max who caught sight of her yellow hard hat lying on the cupboard behind the door.

She watched as he picked it up, and smoothed it thoughtfully with the palm of one hand. He knew as well as she just how much it had cost her in hard work and effort. How much it meant to her. Then he looked up at her, smiling slightly; his eyes were quiet, serious—peaceful. 'Come on,' he said, handing it over to her after a significant little pause. 'It's time we were back out at the rig. We've work to do.'

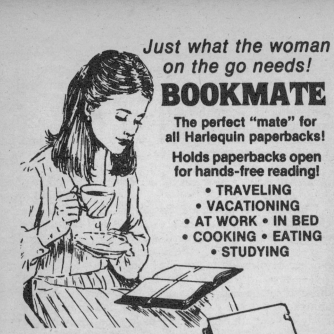

4 FREE

Harlequin Romances

Get all the latest books before they're sold out!

As a Harlequin subscriber you actually receive your personal copies of the latest Romances immediately after they come off the press, so you're sure of getting all 6 each month.

Cancel your subscription whenever you wish!

You don't have to buy any minimum number of books. Whenever you decide to stop your subscription just let us know and we'll cancel all further shipments.

Yours **FREE**, with a home subscription to

HARLEQUIN SUPERROMANCE T.M.

Now you never have to miss reading the newest **HARLEQUIN SUPERROMANCES**... because they'll be delivered right to your door.

Start with your **FREE** LOVE BEYOND DESIRE. You'll be enthralled by this powerful love story...from the moment Robin meets the dark, handsome Carlos and finds herself involved in the jealousies, bitterness and secret passions of the Lopez family. Where her own forbidden love threatens to shatter her life.

Your **FREE** LOVE BEYOND DESIRE is only the beginning. A subscription to **HARLEQUIN SUPERROMANCE** lets you look forward to a long love affair. Month after month, you'll receive four love stories of heroic dimension. Novels that will involve you in spellbinding intrigue, forbidden love and fiery passions.

You'll begin this series of sensuous, exciting contemporary novels...written by some of the top romance novelists of the day...with four every month.

And this big value...each novel, almost 400 pages of compelling reading...is yours for only $2.50 a book. Hours of entertainment every month for so little. Far less than a first-run movie or pay-TV. Newly published novels, with beautifully illustrated covers, filled with page after page of delicious escape into a world of romantic love...delivered right to your home.

Begin a long love affair with

HARLEQUIN SUPERROMANCE.^{T.M.}

Accept LOVE BEYOND DESIRE **FREE.**

Complete and mail the coupon below today!

FREE! Mail to: Harlequin Reader Service

In the U.S.
2504 West Southern Avenue
Tempe, AZ 85282

In Canada
P.O. Box 2800, Postal Station "A"
5170 Yonge St., Willowdale, Ont. M2N 5T5

YES, please send me FREE and without any obligation my
HARLEQUIN SUPERROMANCE novel, LOVE BEYOND DESIRE. If you do
not hear from me after I have examined my FREE book, please send me
the 4 new **HARLEQUIN SUPERROMANCE** books every month as soon
as they come off the press. I understand that I will be billed only $2.50 for
each book (total $10.00). There are no shipping and handling or any
other hidden charges. There is no minimum number of books that I have
to purchase. In fact, I may cancel this arrangement at any time.
LOVE BEYOND DESIRE is mine to keep as a FREE gift, even if I do not
buy any additional books.   134 BPS KAPN

NAME   (Please Print)

ADDRESS   APT. NO.

CITY

STATE/PROV.   ZIP/POSTAL CODE

SIGNATURE (If under 18, parent or guardian must sign.)

SUP-SUB-22

This offer is limited to one order per household and not valid to present
subscribers. Prices subject to change without notice.
Offer expires December 31, 1984